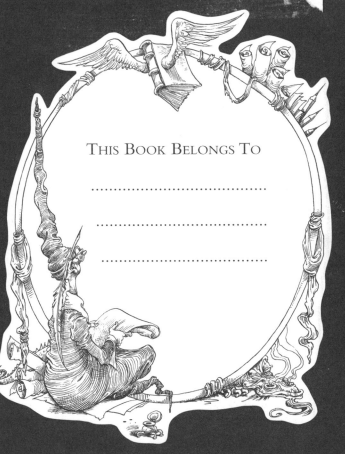

THIS BOOK BELONGS TO

....

....

....

A TREASURY *of* CHILDREN'S CLASSICS

A
TREASURY
of
CHILDREN'S
CLASSICS

VIKING

Published by the Penguin Group
Penguin Books Ltd, 27 Wrights Lane, London W8 5TZ, England
Penguin Putnam Inc., 375 Hudson Street, New York, New York 10014, USA
Penguin Books Australia Ltd, Ringwood, Victoria, Australia
Penguin Books Canada Ltd, 10 Alcorn Avenue, Toronto, Ontario, Canada M4V 3B2
Penguin Books (NZ) Ltd, Private Bag 102902, NSMC, Auckland, New Zealand

Penguin Books Ltd, Registered Offices: Harmondsworth, Middlesex, England

On the World Wide Web at: www.penguin.com

First published as *The Puffin Treasury of Classics* by Viking 1997
This abridged edition published as *A Treasury of Children's Classics* 2000
1 3 5 7 9 10 8 6 4 2

Copyright © Penguin Books Ltd, 1997, 2000
All illustrations remain the copyright © of the individual illustrators credited, 1997
All rights reserved

The moral right of the illustrators has been asserted

Printed in Singapore by Tien Wah Press (PTE) Ltd

Except in the United States of America, this book is sold subject to the condition that it shall not, by way
of trade or otherwise, be lent, re-sold, hired out, or otherwise circulated without the publisher's prior
consent in any form of binding or cover other than that in which it is published and without a similar
condition including this condition being imposed on the subsequent purchaser

British Library Cataloguing in Publication Data
A CIP catalogue record for this book is available from the British Library

ISBN 0–670–89349–8

CONTENTS

Traditional

I SAW A PEACOCK

Illustrated by Emma Chichester Clark

I saw a Peacock with a fiery tail,
I saw a blazing Comet drop down hail,
I saw a Cloud with ivy circled round,
I saw a sturdy Oak creep on the ground,
I saw a Pismire swallow up a whale,
I saw a raging Sea brim full of ale,
I saw a Venice Glass sixteen foot deep,
I saw a Well full of men's tears that weep,
I saw their Eyes all in a flame of fire,
I saw a House as big as the Moon and higher,
I saw the Sun even in the midst of night,
I saw the Man that saw this wondrous sight.

William Shakespeare

When Icicles Hang by the Wall

From

Love's Labour's Lost

Illustrated by Paul Birkbeck

When icicles hang by the wall,
  And Dick the shepherd blows his nail;
When Tom bears logs into the hall,
  And milk comes frozen home in pail;
When blood is nipped, and ways be foul,
– Then nightly sings the staring owl:
  To-who,
To-whit, To-who – a merry note,
While greasy Joan doth keel the pot.

When all aloud the wind doth blow,
  And coughing drowns the parson's saw,
And birds sit brooding in the snow,
  And Marian's nose looks red and raw;
When roasted crabs hiss in the bowl,
– Then nightly sings the staring owl:
  To-who,
To-whit, To-who – a merry note,
While greasy Joan doth keel the pot.

E. Nesbit

FROM

FIVE CHILDREN AND IT

Illustrated by Emma Chichester Clark

'It' is a Sand-fairy the children find one day in a sand-pit.
It grants them one wish a day, lasting until sunset.

Anthea was late for breakfast. It was Robert who quietly poured a spoonful of treacle down the Lamb's frock, so that he had to be taken away and washed thoroughly directly after breakfast. And it was of course a very naughty thing to do; yet it served two purposes – it delighted the Lamb, who loved above all things to be completely sticky, and it engaged Martha's attention so that the others could slip away to the sand-pit without the Lamb.

They did it, and in the lane Anthea, breathless from the scurry of that slipping, panted out –

'I want to propose we take turns to wish. Only, nobody's to have a wish if the others don't think it's a nice wish. Do you agree?'

'Who's to have first wish?' asked Robert cautiously.

'Me, if you don't mind,' said Anthea apologetically. 'And I've thought about it – and it's wings.'

There was a silence. The others rather wanted to find fault, but it was

11

hard, because the word 'wings' raised a flutter of joyous excitement in every breast.

'Not so dusty,' said Cyril generously; and Robert added, 'Really, Panther, you're not quite such a fool as you look.'

Jane said, 'I think it would be perfectly lovely. It's like a bright dream of delirium.'

They found the Sand-fairy easily. Anthea said:

'I wish we all had beautiful wings to fly with.'

The Sand-fairy blew himself out, and next moment each child felt a funny feeling, half heaviness and half lightness, on its shoulders. The Psammead put its head on one side and turned its snail's eyes from one to the other.

'Not so dusty,' it said dreamily. 'But really, Robert, you're not quite such an angel as you look.' Robert almost blushed.

The wings were very big, and more beautiful than you can possibly imagine – for they were soft and smooth, and every feather lay neatly in its place. And the feathers were of the most lovely mixed changing colours, like the rainbow, or iridescent glass, or the beautiful scum that sometimes floats on water that is not at all nice to drink.

'Oh – but can we fly?' Jane said, standing anxiously first on one foot and then on the other.

'Look out!' said Cyril; 'you're treading on my wing.'

'Does it hurt?' asked Anthea with interest; but no one answered, for Robert had spread his wings and jumped up, and now he was slowly rising in the air. He looked very awkward in his knickerbocker suit – his boots in particular hung helplessly, and seemed much larger than when he was standing in them. But the others cared but little how he looked – or how they looked, for that matter.

For now they all spread out their wings and rose in the air. Of course you all know what flying feels like, because everyone has dreamed about flying, and it seems so beautifully easy – only, you can never remember how you did it; and as a rule you have to do it without wings, in your dreams, which is more clever and uncommon, but not so easy to remember the rule for. Now the four children rose flapping from the ground, and you can't think how good the air felt running against their faces. Their wings were tremendously wide when they were spread out, and they had to fly quite a long way apart so as not to get in each other's way. But little things like this are easily learned.

All the words in the English Dictionary, and in the Greek Lexicon as well, are, I find, of no use at all to tell you exactly what it feels like to be flying, so I will not try. But I will say that to look *down* on the fields and woods, instead of *along* at them, is something like looking at a beautiful live map, where, instead of silly colours on paper, you have real moving sunny woods and green fields laid out one after the other. As Cyril said, and I can't think where he got hold of such a strange expression, 'It does you a fair treat!' It was most wonderful and more like real magic than any wish the children had had yet. They flapped and flew and sailed on their great rainbow wings, between green earth and blue sky; and they flew right over Rochester and then swerved round towards Maidstone, and presently they all began to feel extremely hungry. Curiously enough, this happened when they were flying rather low, and just as they were crossing an orchard where some early plums shone red and ripe.

They paused on their wings. I cannot explain to you how this is done, but it is something like treading water when you are swimming, and hawks do it extremely well.

'Yes, I daresay,' said Cyril, though no one had spoken. 'But stealing is stealing even if you've got wings.'

'Do you really think so?' said Jane briskly. 'If you've got wings you're a bird, and no one minds birds breaking the commandments. At least, they may *mind,* but the birds always do it, and no one scolds them or sends them to prison.'

It was not so easy to perch on a plum-tree as you might think, because the rainbow wings were so *very* large; but somehow they all managed to do it, and the plums were certainly very sweet and juicy.

Fortunately, it was not till they had all had quite as many plums as were good for them that they saw a stout man, who looked exactly as though he owned the plum-trees, come hurrying through the orchard gate with a thick stick, and with one accord they disentangled their wings from the plum-laden branches and began to fly.

The man stopped short, with his mouth open. For he had seen the boughs of his trees moving and twitching, and he had said to himself, 'Them young varmints – at it again!' And he had come out at once, for the lads of the village had taught him in past seasons that plums want looking after. But when he saw the rainbow wings flutter up out of the plum-tree he felt that he must have gone quite mad, and he did not like the feeling at all. And when Anthea looked down and saw his mouth go slowly open, and stay so, and his face become green and mauve in patches, she called out:

'Don't be frightened,' and felt hastily in her pocket for a three penny-bit with a hole in it, which she had meant to hang on a ribbon round her neck, for luck. She hovered round the unfortunate plum-owner, and said, 'We have had some of your plums; we thought it wasn't stealing, but now I am not so sure. So here's some money to pay for them.'

She swooped down towards the terror-stricken grower of plums, and

slipped the coin into the pocket of his jacket, and in a few flaps she had rejoined the others.

The farmer sat down on the grass, suddenly and heavily.

'Well – I'm blessed!' he said. 'This here is what they call delusions, I suppose. But this here three-penny' – he had pulled it out and bitten it – '*that's* real enough. Well, from this day forth I'll be a better man. It's the kind of thing to sober a chap for life, this is. I'm glad it was only wings, though. I'd rather see birds as aren't there, and couldn't be, even if they pretend to talk, than some things as I could name.'

He got up slowly and heavily, and went indoors, and he was so nice to his wife that day that she felt quite happy, and said to herself, 'Law, whatever have a-come to the man!' and smartened herself up and put a blue ribbon bow at the place where her collar fastened on, and looked so pretty that he was kinder than ever. So perhaps the winged children really did do one good thing that day. If so, it was the only one; for really there is nothing like wings for getting you into trouble. But, on the other hand, if you are in trouble, there is nothing like wings for getting you out of it.

Robert Louis Stevenson

WINDY NIGHTS

Illustrated by Ian Beck

Whenever the moon and stars are set,
  Whenever the wind is high,
All night long in the dark and wet,
  A man goes riding by.
Late in the night when the fires are out,
Why does he gallop and gallop about?

Whenever the trees are crying aloud,
  And ships are tossed at sea,
By, on the highway, low and loud,
  By at the gallop goes he.
By at the gallop he goes, and then
By he comes back at the gallop again.

Robert Browning

FROM

THE PIED PIPER OF HAMELIN

Illustrated by Siân Bailey

Once more he stepped into the street
 And to his lips again
 Laid his long pipe of smooth straight cane;
And ere he blew three notes (such sweet
Soft notes as yet musician's cunning
 Never gave the enraptured air)
There was a rustling that seemed like a bustling
Of merry crowds justling at pitching and hustling,
Small feet were pattering, wooden shoes clattering,
Little hands clapping and little tongues chattering,
And, like fowls in a farmyard when barley is scattering,
Out came the children running.
All the little boys and girls,
With rosy cheeks and flaxen curls,
And sparkling eyes and teeth like pearls,
Tripping and skipping, ran merrily after
The wonderful music with shouting and laughter.

The Mayor was dumb, and the Council stood
As if they were changed into blocks of wood,
Unable to move a step, or cry
To the children merrily skipping by
– Could only follow with the eye

18

That joyous crowd at the Piper's back.
But how the Mayor was on the rack,
And the wretched Council's bosoms beat,
As the Piper turned from the High Street
To where the Weser rolled its waters
Right in the way of their sons and daughters!
However, he turned from south to west,
And to Koppelberg Hill his steps addressed,
And after him the children pressed;
Great was the joy in every breast.
'He never can cross that mighty top!
He's forced to let the piping drop,
And we shall see our children stop!'
When, lo, as they reached the mountain-side,
A wondrous portal opened wide,
As if a cavern was suddenly hollowed;
And the Piper advanced and the children followed,
And when all were in to the very last,
The door in the mountain-side shut fast.
Did I say, all? No! One was lame,
   And could not dance the whole of the way;
And in after years, if you would blame
   His sadness, he was used to say –
'It's dull in our town since my playmates left!
I can't forget that I'm bereft
Of all the pleasant sights they see,
Which the Piper also promised me.
For he led us, he said, to a joyous land,
Joining the town and just at hand,
Where waters gushed and fruit trees grew
And flowers put forth a fairer hue,
And everything was strange and new;
The sparrows were brighter than peacocks here,

19

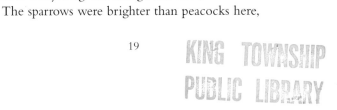

And their dogs outran our fallow deer,
And honey-bees had lost their stings,
And horses were born with eagles' wings:
And just as I became assured
My lame foot would be speedily cured,
The music stopped and I stood still,
And found myself outside the hill,
Left alone against my will,
To go now limping as before,
And never hear of that country more!'

William Shakespeare

WHERE THE BEE SUCKS

Illustrated by Paul Birkbeck

Where the bee sucks, there suck I,
In a cowslip's bell I lie,
There I couch when owls do cry.
On the bat's back I do fly
After summer merrily.
Merrily, merrily shall I live now
Under the blossom that hangs on the bough.

Lewis Carroll

From

THROUGH THE
LOOKING-GLASS

Illustrated by Chris Riddell

*When Alice steps through the looking-glass,
she enters a world of chess pieces and nursery-rhyme
characters who behave very oddly.*

They were standing under a tree, each with an arm round the other's neck, and Alice knew which was which in a moment, because one of them had 'DUM' embroidered on his collar, and the other 'DEE'. 'I suppose they've each got "TWEEDLE" round at the back of the collar,' she said to herself.

They stood so still that she quite forgot they were alive, and she was just looking round to see if the word 'TWEEDLE' was written at the back of each collar, when she was startled by a voice coming from the one marked 'DUM'.

'If you think we're wax-works,' he said, 'you ought to pay, you know. Wax-works weren't made to be looked at for nothing. Nohow!'

'Contrariwise,' added the one marked 'DEE', 'if you think we're alive, you ought to speak.'

'I'm sure I'm very sorry,' was all Alice could say; for the words of the old song kept ringing through her head like the ticking of a clock, and she could hardly help saying them out loud: –

'Tweedledum and Tweedledee
Agreed to have a battle;
For Tweedledum said Tweedledee
Had spoiled his nice new rattle.

Just then flew down a monstrous crow,
As black as a tar-barrel;
Which frightened both the heroes so,
They quite forgot their quarrel.'

'I know what you're thinking about,' said Tweedledum: 'but it isn't so, nohow.'

'Contrariwise,' continued Tweedledee, 'if it was so, it might be; and if it were so, it would be; but as it isn't, it ain't. That's logic.'

'I was thinking,' Alice said very politely, 'which is the best way out of this wood: it's getting so dark. Would you tell me, please?'

But the fat little men only looked at each other and grinned.

They looked so exactly like a couple of great schoolboys, that Alice couldn't help pointing her finger at Tweedledum, and saying 'First Boy!'

'Nohow!' Tweedledum cried out briskly, and shut his mouth up again with a snap.

'Next Boy!' said Alice, passing on to Tweedledee, though she felt quite certain he would only shout out 'Contrariwise!' and so he did.

'You've begun wrong!' cried Tweedledum. 'The first thing in a visit is to say "How d'ye do?" and shake hands!' And here the two brothers gave each other a hug, and then they held out the two hands that were free, to shake hands with her.

Alice did not like shaking hands with either of them first, for fear of hurting the other one's feelings; so, as the best way out of the difficulty, she took hold of both hands at once: the next moment they were dancing round in a ring. This seemed quite natural (she

remembered afterwards), and she was not even surprised to hear music playing: it seemed to come from the tree under which they were dancing and it was done (as well as she could make it out) by the branches rubbing one across the other, like fiddles and fiddle-sticks.

'But it certainly *was* funny,' (Alice said afterwards, when she was telling her sister the history of all this,) 'to find myself singing "*Here we go round the mulberry bush*". I don't know when I began it, but somehow I felt as if I'd been singing it a long long time!'

The other two dancers were fat, and very soon out of breath. 'Four times round is enough for one dance,' Tweedledum panted out, and they left off dancing as suddenly as they had begun: the music stopped at the same moment.

Then they let go of Alice's hands, and stood looking at her for a minute: there was a rather awkward pause, as Alice didn't know how to begin a conversation with people she had just been dancing with. 'It would never do to say "How d'ye do?" now,' she said to herself: 'we seem to have got beyond that, somehow!'

'I hope you're not much tired?' she said at last.

'Nohow. And thank you very much for asking,' said Tweedledum.

'So *much* obliged!' added Tweedledee. 'You like poetry?'

'Ye-es, pretty well – some poetry,' Alice said doubtfully. 'Would you tell me which road leads out of the wood?'

'What shall I repeat to her?' said Tweedledee, looking round at Tweedledum with great solemn eyes, and not noticing Alice's question.

' "*The Walrus and the Carpenter*" is the longest,' Tweedledum replied, giving his brother an affectionate hug.

Tweedledee began instantly:

'The sun was shining –'

Here Alice ventured to interrupt him. 'If it's *very* long,' she said, as politely as she could, 'would you please tell me first which road –'

Tweedledee smiled gently, and began again:

'The sun was shining on the sea,
  Shining with all his might:
He did his very best to make
  The billows smooth and bright –
And this was odd, because it was
  The middle of the night.

The moon was shining sulkily,
  Because she thought the sun
Had got no business to be there
  After the day was done –
"It's very rude of him," she said,
  "To come and spoil the fun!"

The sea was wet as wet could be,
  The sands were dry as dry.
You could not see a cloud, because
  No cloud was in the sky:
No birds were flying overhead –
  There were no birds to fly.

The Walrus and the Carpenter
  Were walking close at hand;
They wept like anything to see
  Such quantities of sand:
"If this were only cleared away,"
  They said, "it would be grand!"

"If seven maids with seven mops
  Swept it for half a year,
Do you suppose," the Walrus said,
  "That they could get it clear?"
"I doubt it," said the Carpenter,
  And shed a bitter tear.

"O Oysters, come and walk with us!"
  The Walrus did beseech.
"A pleasant walk, a pleasant talk,
  Along the briny beach:
We cannot do with more than four,
  To give a hand to each."

The eldest Oyster looked at him.
  But never a word he said:
The eldest Oyster winked his eye,
  And shook his heavy head –
Meaning to say he did not choose
  To leave the oyster-bed.

But four young Oysters hurried up,
  All eager for the treat:
Their coats were brushed, their faces washed,
  Their shoes were clean and neat –
And this was odd, because, you know,
  They hadn't any feet.

Four other Oysters followed them,
  And yet another four;
And thick and fast they came at last,
  And more, and more, and more –
All hopping through the frothy waves,
  And scrambling to the shore.

The Walrus and the Carpenter
  Walked on a mile or so,
And then they rested on a rock
  Conveniently low:
And all the little Oysters stood
  And waited in a row.

"The time has come," the Walrus said,
  "To talk of many things:
Of shoes – and ships – and sealing-wax –
  Of cabbages – and kings –
And why the sea is boiling hot –
  And whether pigs have wings."

"But wait a bit," the Oysters cried,
  "Before we have our chat;
For some of us are out of breath,
  And all of us are fat!"
"No hurry!" said the Carpenter.
  They thanked him much for that.

"A loaf of bread," the Walrus said,
  "Is what we chiefly need:
Pepper and vinegar besides
  Are very good indeed –
Now if you're ready, Oysters dear,
  We can begin to feed."

"But not on us!" the Oysters cried,
Turning a little blue.
"After such kindness, that would be
A dismal thing to do!"
"The night is fine," the Walrus said.
"Do you admire the view?

"It was so kind of you to come!
And you are very nice!"
The Carpenter said nothing but
"Cut us another slice:
I wish you were not quite so deaf –
I've had to ask you twice!"

"It seems a shame," the Walrus said,
"To play them such a trick,
After we've brought them out so far,
And made them trot so quick!"
The Carpenter said nothing but
"The butter's spread too thick!"

"I weep for you," the Walrus said,
"I deeply sympathize."
With sobs and tears he sorted out
Those of the largest size,
Holding his pocket-handkerchief
Before his streaming eyes.

"O Oysters," said the Carpenter.
"You've had a pleasant run!
Shall we be trotting home again?"
But answer came there none –
And this was scarcely odd, because
They'd eaten every one.'

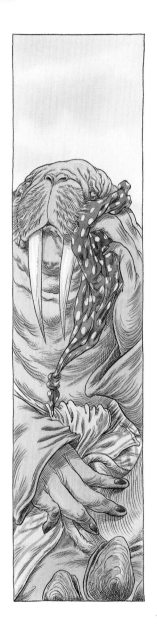

29

'I like the Walrus best,' said Alice: 'because you see he was a *little* sorry for the poor oysters.'

'He ate more than the Carpenter, though,' said Tweedledee. 'You see he held his handkerchief in front, so that the Carpenter couldn't count how many he took: contrariwise.'

'That was mean!' Alice said indignantly. 'Then I like the Carpenter best – if he didn't eat so many as the Walrus.'

'But he ate as many as he could get,' said Tweedledum.

This was a puzzler. After a pause, Alice began, 'Well! They were *both* very unpleasant characters –' Here she checked herself in some alarm, at hearing something that sounded to her like the puffing of a large steam-engine in the wood near them, though she feared it was more likely to be a wild beast. 'Are there any lions or tigers about here?' she asked timidly.

'It's only the Red King snoring,' said Tweedledee.

'Come and look at him!' the brothers cried, and they took each one of Alice's hands, and led her up to where the King was sleeping.

'Isn't he a *lovely* sight?' said Tweedledum.

Alice couldn't say honestly that he was. He had a tall red night-cap on, with a tassel, and he was lying crumpled up into a sort of untidy heap, and snoring loud – 'fit to snore his head off!' as Tweedledum remarked.

'I'm afraid he'll catch cold with lying on the damp grass,' said Alice, who was a very thoughtful little girl.

'He's dreaming now,' said Tweedledee: 'and what do you think he's dreaming about?'

Alice said, 'Nobody can guess that.'

'Why, about *you*!' Tweedledee exclaimed, clapping his hands triumphantly. 'And if he left off dreaming about you, where do you suppose you'd be?'

'Where I am now, of course,' said Alice.

'Not you!' Tweedledee retorted contemptuously. 'You'd be nowhere. Why, you're only a sort of thing in his dream!'

'If that there King was to wake,' added Tweedledum, 'you'd go out –

bang! – just like a candle!'

'I shouldn't!' Alice exclaimed indignantly. 'Besides, if *I'm* only a sort of thing in his dream, what are *you*, I should like to know?'

'Ditto,' said Tweedledum.

'Ditto, ditto!' cried Tweedledee.

He shouted this so loud that Alice couldn't help saying, 'Hush! You'll be waking him, I'm afraid, if you make so much noise.'

'Well, it's no use *your* talking about waking him,' said Tweedledum, 'when you're only one of the things in his dream. You know very well you're not real.'

'I *am* real!' said Alice, and began to cry.

'You won't make yourself a bit realler by crying,' Tweedledee remarked: 'there's nothing to cry about.'

'If I wasn't real,' Alice said – half-laughing through her tears, it all seemed so ridiculous – 'I shouldn't be able to cry.'

'I hope you don't suppose those are real tears?' Tweedledum interrupted in a tone of great contempt.

'I know they're talking nonsense,' Alice thought to herself: 'and it's foolish to cry about it.' So she brushed away her tears, and went on as cheerfully as she could, 'At any rate I'd better be getting out of the wood, for really it's coming on very dark. Do you think it's going to rain?'

Tweedledum spread a large umbrella over himself and his brother, and looked up into it. 'No, I don't think it is,' he said: 'at least – not under *here*. Nohow.'

'But it may rain *outside*?'

'It may – if it chooses,' said Tweedledee: 'we've no objection. Contrariwise.'

'Selfish things!' thought Alice, and she was just going to say 'Good-night' and leave them, when Tweedledum sprang out from under the umbrella, and seized her by the wrist.

'Do you see *that?*' he said, in a voice choking with passion, and his eyes grew large and yellow all in a moment, as he pointed with a trembling finger at a small white thing lying under the tree.

'It's only a rattle,' Alice said, after a careful examination of the little white thing. 'Not a rattle*snake*, you know,' she added hastily, thinking that he was frightened: 'only an old rattle – quite old and broken.'

'I knew it was!' cried Tweedledum, beginning to stamp about wildly and tear his hair. 'It's spoilt, of course!' Here he looked at Tweedledee, who immediately sat down on the ground, and tried to hide himself under the umbrella.

Alice laid her hand upon his arm, and said in a soothing tone, 'You needn't be so angry about an old rattle.'

'But it isn't old!' Tweedledum cried, in a greater fury than ever. 'It's new, I tell you – I bought it yesterday – my nice NEW RATTLE!' and his voice rose to a perfect scream.

All this time Tweedledee was trying his best to fold up the umbrella, with himself in it: which was such an extraordinary thing to do, that it quite took off Alice's attention from the angry brother. But he couldn't quite succeed, and it ended in his rolling over, bundled up in the umbrella, with only his head out: and there he lay, opening and shutting his mouth and his large eyes – 'looking more like a fish than anything else,' Alice thought.

'Of course you agree to have a battle?' Tweedledum said in a calmer tone.

'I suppose so,' the other sulkily replied, as he crawled out of the umbrella: 'only *she* must help us to dress up, you know.'

So the two brothers went off hand-in-hand into the wood, and returned in a minute with their arms full of things – such as bolsters, blankets, hearth-rugs, table-cloths, dish-covers and coal-scuttles. 'I hope you're a good hand at pinning and tying strings?' Tweedledum remarked. 'Every one of these things has got to go on, somehow or other.'

Alice said afterwards she had never seen such a fuss made about anything in all her life – the way those two bustled about – and the quantity of things they put on – and the trouble they gave her in tying strings and fastening buttons – 'Really they'll be more like bundles of old clothes than anything else, by the time they're ready!' she said to herself, as she arranged a bolster round the neck of Tweedledee, 'to keep his head from being cut off,' as he said.

'You know,' he added very gravely, 'it's one of the most serious things that can possibly happen to one in a battle – to get one's head cut off.'

Alice laughed loud: but she managed to turn it into a cough, for fear of hurting his feelings.

'Do I look very pale?' said Tweedledum, coming up to have his helmet tied on. (He *called* it a helmet, though it certainly looked much more like a saucepan.)

'Well – yes – a *little*,' Alice replied gently.

'I'm very brave generally,' he went on in a low voice: 'only today I happen to have a headache.'

'And *I've* got a toothache!' said Tweedledee, who had overheard the remark. 'I'm far worse than you!'

'Then you'd better not fight to-day,' said Alice thinking it a good opportunity to make peace.

'We *must* have a bit of a fight, but I don't care about going on long,' said Tweedledum. 'What's the time now?'

Tweedledee looked at his watch, and said, 'Half-past four.'

'Let's fight till six, and then have dinner,' said Tweedledum.

'Very well,' the other said, rather sadly: 'and *she* can watch us – only you'd better not come *very* close,' he added: 'I generally hit everything I can see – when I get really excited.'

'And *I* hit everything within reach,' cried Tweedledum, 'whether I can see it or not.'

Alice laughed. 'You must hit the *trees* pretty often, I should think,' she said.

Tweedledum looked round him with a satisfied smile. 'I don't suppose,' he said, 'there'll be a tree left standing, for ever so far round, by the time we've finished!'

'And all about a rattle!' said Alice still hoping to make them a *little* ashamed of fighting for such a trifle.

'I shouldn't have minded it so much,' said Tweedledum, 'if it hadn't been a new one.'

'I wish the monstrous crow would come!' thought Alice.

'There's only one sword, you know,' Tweedledum said to his brother: 'but you can have the umbrella – it's quite as sharp Only we must begin quick. It's getting as dark as it can.'

'And darker,' said Tweedledee.

It was getting dark so suddenly that Alice thought there must be a thunderstorm coming on. 'What a thick black cloud that is!' she said. 'And how fast it comes! Why, I do believe it's got wings!'

'It's the crow!' Tweedledum cried out in a shrill voice of alarm: and the two brothers took to their heels and were out of sight in a moment.

Alice ran a little way into the wood, and stopped under a large tree. 'It can never get at me *here*,' she thought: 'it's far too large to squeeze itself in among the trees. But I wish it wouldn't flap its wings so – it makes quite a hurricane in the wood – here's somebody's shawl being blown away!'

Percy Bysshe Shelley

OZYMANDIAS

Illustrated by Anthony Browne

I met a traveller from an antique land
Who said: Two vast and trunkless legs of stone
Stand in the desert. Near them, on the sand,
Half sunk, a shattered visage lies, whose frown,
And wrinkled lip, and sneer of cold command,
Tell that its sculptor well those passions read
Which yet survive (stamped on these lifeless things),
The hand that mocked them and the heart that fed;
And on the pedestal these words appear:
'My name is Ozymandias, king of kings;
Look on my works, ye Mighty, and despair!'
Nothing beside remains. Round the decay
Of that colossal wreck, boundless and bare,
The lone and level sands stretch far away.

William Wordsworth

DAFFODILS

Illustrated by Ruth Rivers

I wander'd lonely as a cloud
  That floats on high o'er vales and hills,
When all at once I saw a crowd,
  A host of golden daffodils;
Beside the lake, beneath the trees,
Fluttering and dancing in the breeze.

Continuous as the stars that shine
  And twinkle on the Milky Way,
They stretch'd in never-ending line
  Along the margin of a bay:
Ten thousand saw I at a glance,
Tossing their heads in sprightly dance.

The waves beside them danced, but they
  Out-did the sparkling waves in glee:
A poet could not but be gay,
  In such a jocund company:
I gazed – and gazed – but little thought
What wealth the show to me had brought:

For oft, when on my couch I lie
  In vacant or in pensive mood,
They flash upon that inward eye
  Which is the bliss of solitude;
And then my heart with pleasure fills,
And dances with the daffodils.

Jack London

FROM

THE CALL OF THE WILD

Illustrated by John Butler

*Buck is a dog born to luxury, but betrayed and sold to be a
sledge dog in the harsh and frozen Yukon.*

Buck's first day on the Dyea beach was like a nightmare. Every hour was filled with shock and surprise. He had been suddenly jerked from the heart of civilization and flung into the heart of things primordial. No lazy, sunkissed life was this, with nothing to do but loaf and be bored. Here was neither peace, nor rest, nor a moment's safety. All was confusion and action, and every moment life and limb were in peril. There was imperative need to be constantly alert; for these dogs and men were not town dogs and men. They were savages, all of them; who knew no law but the law of club and fang.

He had never seen dogs fight as these wolfish creatures fought, and his first experience taught him an unforgettable lesson. It is true, it was a vicarious experience, else he would not have lived to profit by it. Curly was the victim. They were camped near the log store, where she, in her friendly way, made advances to a husky dog the size of a full-grown wolf, though not half so large as she. There was no warning, only a leap in like a flash, a metallic clip of teeth, a leap out equally swift, and Curly's face was ripped open from eye to jaw.

It was the wolf manner of fighting, to strike and leap away; but there was more to it than this. Thirty or forty huskies ran to the spot and surrounded the combatants in an intent and silent circle. Buck did not comprehend that silent intentness, nor the eager way with which they were licking their chops. Curly rushed her antagonist, who struck again and leaped aside. He met her next rush with his chest, in a peculiar fashion that tumbled her off her feet. She never regained them. This was what the onlooking huskies had waited for. They closed in upon her, snarling and yelping, and she was buried, screaming with agony, beneath the bristling mass of bodies.

So sudden was it, and so unexpected, that Buck was taken aback. He saw Spitz run out his scarlet tongue in a way he had of laughing; and he saw François swinging an axe, spring into the mess of dogs. Three men with clubs were helping him to scatter them. It did not take long. Two minutes from the time Curly went down, the last of her assailants were clubbed off. But she lay there limp and lifeless in the bloody, trampled snow, almost literally torn to pieces, the swart half-breed standing over her and cursing horribly. The scene often came back to Buck to trouble him in his sleep. So that was the way. No fair play. Once down, that was the end of you. Well, he would see to it that he never went down. Spitz ran out his tongue and laughed again and from that moment Buck hated him with a bitter and deathless hatred.

Before he had recovered from the shock caused by the tragic passing of Curly, he received another shock. François fastened upon him an arrangement of straps and buckles. It was a harness, such as he had seen the grooms put on the horses at home. And as he had seen horses work, so he was set to work, hauling François on a sled to the forest that fringed the valley, and returning with a load of firewood. Though his dignity was sorely hurt by thus being made a draught animal, he was too wise to rebel. He buckled down with a will and did his best, though it was all new and strange. François was stern, demanding instant obedience; and by virtue of his whip receiving instant obedience; while Dave, who was an experienced wheeler, nipped Buck's hindquarters whenever he was in error. Spitz was the leader, likewise experienced, and while he could not always get at Buck, he growled sharp reproof now and again, or cunningly threw his weight in the traces to jerk Buck into the way he should go. Buck learned easily, and under the combined tuition of his two mates and François made remarkable progress. Ere they returned to camp he knew enough to stop at 'ho', to go ahead at 'mush', to swing wide on the bends; and to keep clear of the wheeler when the loaded sled shot downhill at their heels.

'T'ree vair' good dogs,' François told Perrault. 'Dat Buck, heem pool lak hell, I tich heem queek as anyt'ing.'

By afternoon, Perrault, who was in a hurry to be on the trail with his dispatches, returned with two more dogs. 'Billee' and 'Joe' he called them, two brothers, and true huskies both. Sons of the one mother though they were, they were as different as day and night. Billee's one fault was his excessive good nature, while Joe was the very opposite, sour and introspective, with a perpetual snarl and a malignant eye. Buck received them in comradely fashion. Dave ignored them; while Spitz proceeded to thrash first one and then the other. Billee wagged his tail appeasingly, turned to run when he saw that appeasement was of no avail, and cried (still appeasingly) when Spitz's sharp teeth scored his flank. But no matter how Spitz circled, Joe whirled around on his heels to face him, mane bristling, ears laid back, lips writhing and snarling, jaws clipping together as fast as he could snap, and eyes diabolically gleaming – the incarnation of belligerent fear. So terrible was his appearance that Spitz was forced to forego disciplining him; but to cover his own discomfiture he turned upon the inoffensive and wailing Billee and drove him to the confines of the camp.

By evening Perrault secured another dog, an old husky, long and

lean and gaunt, with a battle-scarred face and a single eye which flashed a warning of prowess that commanded respect. He was called Sol-leks, which means the Angry One. Like Dave, he asked nothing, gave nothing, expected nothing; and when he marched slowly and deliberately into their midst, even Spitz left him alone. He had one peculiarity which Buck was unlucky enough to discover. He did not like to be approached on his blind side. Of this offence Buck was unwittingly guilty, and the first knowledge he had of his indiscretion was when Sol-leks whirled upon him and slashed his shoulder to the bone for three inches up and down. Forever after Buck avoided his blind side, and to the last of their comradeship had no more trouble. His only apparent ambition, like Dave's, was to be left alone; though, as Buck was afterward to learn, each of them possessed one other and even more vital ambition.

That night Buck faced the great problem of sleeping. The tent, illumined by a candle, glowed warmly in the midst of the white plain; and when he, as a matter of course, entered it, both Perrault and François bombarded him with curses and cooking utensils till he recovered from his consternation and fled ignominiously into the outer cold. A chill wind was blowing that nipped him sharply and bit with especial venom into his wounded shoulder. He lay down on the snow and attempted to sleep, but the frost soon drove him shivering to his feet. Miserable and disconsolate, he wandered about among the

many tents, only to find that one place was as cold as another. Here and there savage dogs rushed upon him, but he bristled his neck-hair and snarled (for he was learning fast), and they let him go his way unmolested.

Finally an idea came to him. He would return and see how his own team-mates were making out. To his astonishment, they had disappeared. Again he wandered about through the great camp, looking for them, and again he returned. Were they in the tent? No, that could not be, else he would not have been driven out. Then where could they possibly be? With dropping tail and shivering body, very forlorn indeed, he aimlessly circled the tent. Suddenly the snow gave way beneath his fore legs and he sank down. Something wriggled under his feet. He sprang back, bristling and snarling, fearful of the unseen and unknown. But a friendly little yelp reassured him, and he went back to investigate. A whiff of warm air ascended to his nostrils, and there, curled up under the snow in a snug ball, lay Billee. He whined placatingly, squirmed and wriggled to show his good will and intention, and even ventured, as a bribe for peace, to lick Buck's face with his warm wet tongue.

Another lesson. So that was the way they did it, eh? Buck confidently selected a spot, and with much fuss and wasted effort proceeded to dig a hole for himself. In a trice the heat from his body filled the confined space and he was asleep.

James Hogg

A BOY'S SONG

Illustrated by Tim Clarey

Where the pools are bright and deep,
Where the grey trout lies asleep,
Up the river and over the lea –
That's the way for Billy and me.

Where the blackbird sings the latest,
Where the hawthorn blooms the sweetest,
Where the nestlings chirp and flee,
That's the way for Billy and me.

Where the mowers mow the cleanest,
Where the hay lies thick and greenest;
There to trace the homeward bee,
That's the way for Billy and me.

Where the hazel bank is steepest,
Where the shadow falls the deepest,
Where the clustering nuts fall free,
That's the way for Billy and me.

Why the boys should drive away
Little sweet maidens from their play,
Or love to banter and fight so well,
That's the thing I never could tell.

But this I know, I love to play,
Through the meadow, among the hay;
Up the water and over the lea,
That's the way for Billy and me.

Robert Louis Stevenson

FROM

TREASURE ISLAND

Illustrated by Richard Jones

Jim Hawkins, cabin-boy on the Hispaniola, *overhears
Long John Silver plotting a mutiny.*

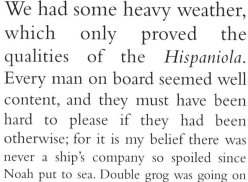

We had some heavy weather, which only proved the qualities of the *Hispaniola*. Every man on board seemed well content, and they must have been hard to please if they had been otherwise; for it is my belief there was never a ship's company so spoiled since Noah put to sea. Double grog was going on the least excuse; there was duff on odd days, as, for instance, if the squire heard it was any man's birthday; and always a barrel of apples standing broached in the waist, for anyone to help himself that had a fancy.

'Never knew good come of it yet,' the captain said to Dr Livesey. 'Spoil foc's'le hands, make devils. That's my belief.'

But good did come of the apple barrel, as you shall hear; for if it had not been for that, we should have had no note of warning, and might all have perished by the hand of treachery.

This was how it came about.

We had run up the trades to get the wind of the island we were after

48

– I am not allowed to be more plain – and now we were ru ..ing down for it with a bright look-out day and night. It was about the last day of our outward voyage, by the largest computation; some time that night, or, at latest, before noon of the morrow, we should sight the Treasure Island. We were heading SSW., and had a steady breeze abeam and a quiet sea. The *Hispaniola* rolled steadily, dipping her bowsprit now and then with a whiff of spray. All was drawing alow and aloft; everyone was in the bravest spirits, because we were now so near an end of the first part of our adventure.

Now, just after sundown, when all my work was over and I was on my way to my berth, it occurred to me that I should like an apple. I ran on deck. The watch was all forward looking out for the island. The man at the helm was watching the luff of the sail, and whistling away gently to himself; and that was the only sound excepting the swish of the sea against the bows and around the sides of the ship.

In I got bodily into the apple barrel, and found there was scarce an apple left; but, sitting down there in the dark, what with the sound of the waters and the rocking movement of the ship, I had either fallen asleep, or was on the point of doing so, when a heavy man sat down with rather a clash close by. The barrel shook as he leaned his shoulders against it, and I was just about to jump up when the man began to speak. It was Silver's voice, and, before

I had heard a dozen words, I would not have shown myself for all the world, but lay there, trembling and listening, in the extreme of fear and curiosity; for from these dozen words I understood that the lives of all the honest men aboard depended upon me alone.

'No, not I,' said Silver. 'Flint was cap'n; I was quartermaster, along of my timber leg. The same broadside I lost my leg, old Pew lost his deadlights. It was a master surgeon, him that ampytated me – out of college and all – Latin by the bucket, and what not; but he was hanged like a dog, and sun-dried like the rest, at Corso Castle. That was Roberts' men, that was, and comed of changing names of their ships – *Royal Fortune* and so on. Now, what a ship was christened, so let her stay, I says. So it was with the *Cassandra*, as brought us all safe home from Malabar, after England took the Viceroy of the Indies; so it was with the old *Walrus*, Flint's old ship, as I've seen a'muck with the red blood and fit to sink with gold.'

'Ah!' cried another voice, that of the youngest hand on board, and evidently full of admiration, 'he was the flower of the flock, was Flint!'

'Davis was a man, too, by all accounts,' said Silver. 'I never sailed along of him; first with England, then with Flint, that's my story; and now here on my own account, in a manner of speaking. I laid by nine hundred safe, from England, and two thousand after Flint. That ain't bad for a man before the mast – all safe in bank. 'Tain't earning now, it's saving does it, you may lay to that. Where's all England's men now? I dunno. Where's Flint's? Why, most on 'em aboard here, and glad to get the duff – been begging before that, some on 'em. Old Pew, as had lost his sight, and might have thought shame, spends twelve hundred pounds in a year, like a lord in Parliament. Where is he now? Well, he's dead now and under hatches; but for two year before that, shiver my timbers! the man was starving. He begged, and he stole, and he cut throats, and starved at that, by the powers!'

'Well, it ain't much use, after all,' said the young seaman.

''Tain't much use for fools, you may lay to it – that, nor nothing,' cried Silver. 'But now, you look here: you're young, you are, but you're as smart as paint. I see that when I set my eyes on you, and I'll talk to you like a man.'

You may imagine how I felt when I heard this abominable old rogue addressing another in the very same words of flattery as he had used to myself. I think, if I had been able, that I would have killed him through the barrel. Meantime, he ran on, little supposing he was overheard.

'Here it is about gentlemen of fortune. They lives rough, and they risk swinging, but they eat and drink like fighting-cocks, and when a cruise is done, why it's hundreds of pounds instead of hundreds of farthings in their pockets. Now, the most goes for rum and a good fling, and to sea again in their shirts. But that's not the course I lay. I puts it all away, some here, some there, and none too much anywheres, by reason of suspicion. I'm fifty, mark you; once back from this cruise, I set up gentleman in earnest. Time enough, too, says you. Ah, but I've lived easy in the meantime; never denied myself o' nothing heart desires, and slep' soft and ate dainty all my days, but when at sea. And how did I begin? Before the mast, like you!'

'Well,' said the other, 'but all the other money's gone now, ain't it? You daren't show face in Bristol after this.'

'Why, where might you suppose it was?' asked Silver, derisively.

'At Bristol, in banks and places,' answered his companion.

'It were,' said the cook; 'it were when we weighed anchor. But my old missis has it all by now. And the "Spy-glass" is sold, lease and goodwill and rigging; and the old girl's off to meet me. I would tell you where, for I trust you; but it 'ud make jealousy among the mates.'

'And can you trust your missis?' asked the other.

'Gentlemen of fortune,' returned the cook, 'usually trust little among themselves, and right they are, you may lay to it. But I have a way with me, I have. When a mate brings a slip on his cable – one as knows me, I mean – it won't be in the same world with old John. There was some that was feared of Pew, and some that was feared of Flint; but Flint his own self was feared of me. Feared he was, and proud. They was the roughest crew afloat, was Flint's; the devil himself would have been

feared to go to sea with them. Well, now, I tell you, I'm not a boasting man, and you seen yourself how easy I keep company; but when I was quartermaster, *lambs* wasn't the word for Flint's old buccaneers. Ah, you may be sure of yourself in old John's ship.'

'Well, I tell you now,' replied the lad, 'I didn't half a quarter like the job till I had this talk with you, John; but there's my hand on it now.'

'And a brave lad you were, and smart, too,' answered Silver, shaking hands so heartily that all the barrel shook, 'and a finer figurehead for a gentleman of fortune I never clapped my eyes on.'

By this time I had begun to understand the meaning of their terms. By a 'gentleman of fortune' they plainly meant neither more nor less than a common pirate, and the little scene that I had overheard was the last act in the corruption of one of the honest hands – perhaps of the last one left aboard. But on this point I was soon to be relieved, for Silver giving a little whistle, a third man strolled up and sat down by the party.

'Dick's square,' said Silver.

'Oh, I know'd Dick was square,' returned the voice of the coxswain, Israel Hands. 'He's no fool, is Dick.' And he turned his quid and spat. 'But, look here,' he went on, 'here's what I want to know, Barbecue: how long are we a-going to stand off and on like a blessed bumboat? I've had a'most enough o' Cap'n Smollett; he's hazed me long enough, by thunder! I want to go into that cabin, I do. I want their pickles and wines, and that.'

'Israel,' said Silver, 'your head ain't much account, nor ever was. But you're able to hear, I reckon; leastways, your ears is big enough. Now, here's what I say: you'll berth forward, and you'll live hard, and you'll speak soft, and you'll keep sober, till I give the word; and you may lay to that, old son.'

'Well, I don't say no, do I?' growled the coxswain. 'What I say is, when? That's what I say.'

'When! by the powers!' cried Silver. 'Well, now, if you want to know, I'll tell you when. The last moment I can manage; and that's when. Here's a first-rate seaman, Cap'n Smollett, sails the blessed ship for us.

Here's this squire and doctor with a map and such – I don't know where it is, do I? No more do you, says you. Well, then, I mean this squire and doctor shall find the stuff, and help us to get it aboard, by the powers. Then we'll see. If I was sure of you all, sons of double Dutchmen, I'd have Cap'n Smollett navigate us half-way back again before I struck.'

'Why, we're all seamen aboard here, I should think,' said the lad Dick.

'We're all foc's'le hands, you mean,' snapped Silver. 'We can steer a course, but who's to set one? That's what all you gentlemen split on, first and last. If I had my way, I'd have Cap'n Smollett work us back into the trades at least; then we'd have no blessed miscalculations and a spoonful of water a day. But I know the sort you are. I'll finish with 'em at the island, as soon's the blunt's on board, and a pity it is. But you're never happy till you're drunk. Split my sides, I've a sick heart to sail with the likes of you!'

'Easy all, Long John,' cried Israel. 'Who's a-crossin' of you?'

'Why, how many tall ships, think ye, now, have I seen laid aboard? and how many brisk lads drying in the sun at Execution Dock?' cried Silver, 'and all for this same hurry and hurry and hurry. You hear me? I seen a thing or two at sea, I have. If you would on'y lay your course, and a p'int to windward, you would ride in carriages, you would. But not you! I know you. You'll have your mouthful of rum tomorrow, and go hang.'

'Everybody know'd you was a kind of a chapling, John; but there's others as could hand and steer as well as you,' said Israel. 'They liked a bit of fun, they did. They wasn't so high and dry, nohow, but took their fling, like jolly companions every one.'

'So?' says Silver. 'Well, and where

are they now? Pew was that sort, and he died a beggar-man. Flint was, and he died of rum at Savannah. Ah, they was a sweet crew, they was! on'y, where are they?'

'But,' asked Dick, 'when we do lay 'em athwart, what are we to do with 'em, anyhow?'

'There's the man for me!' cried the cook, admiringly. 'That's what I call business. Well, what would you think? Put 'em ashore like maroons? That would have been England's way. Or cut 'em down like that much pork? That would have been Flint's or Billy Bones's.'

'Billy was the man for that,' said Israel. ' "Dead men don't bite," says he. Well, he's dead now hisself; he knows the long and short of it now; and if ever a rough hand come to port, it was Billy.'

'Right you are,' said Silver, 'rough and ready. But mark you here: I'm an easy man – I'm quite the gentleman, says you; but this time it's serious. Dooty is dooty, mates. I give my vote – death. When I'm in Parlyment, and riding in my coach, I don't want none of these sea-lawyers in the cabin a-coming home, unlooked for, like the devil at prayers. Wait is what I say; but when the time comes, why let her rip!'

'John,' cries the coxswain, 'you're a man!'

'You'll say so, Israel, when you see,' said Silver. 'Only one thing I claim – I claim Trelawney. I'll wring his calf's head off his body with these hands. Dick!' he added, breaking off, 'you just jump up, like a sweet lad, and get me an apple, to wet my pipe like.'

You may fancy the terror I was in! I should have leaped out and run for it, if I had found the strength; but my limbs and heart alike misgave me. I heard Dick begin to rise, and then someone seemingly stopped him, and the voice of Hands exclaimed:

'Oh, stow that! Don't you get sucking of that bilge, John. Let's have a go of the rum.'

'Dick,' said Silver, 'I trust you. I've a gauge on the keg, mind. There's the key; you fill a pannikin and bring it up.'

Terrified as I was, I could not help thinking to myself that this must have been how Mr Arrow got the strong waters that destroyed him.

Dick was gone but a little while, and during his absence Israel spoke straight on in the cook's ear. It was but a word or two that I could catch, and yet I gathered some important news; for, besides other scraps that tended to the same purpose, this whole clause was audible: 'Not another man of them'll jine.' Hence there were still faithful men on board.

When Dick returned, one after another of the trio took the pannikin and drank – one 'To luck'; another with a 'Here's to old Flint'; and Silver himself saying, in a kind of song, 'Here's to ourselves, and hold your luff, plenty of prizes and plenty of duff.'

Just then a sort of brightness fell upon me in the barrel, and, looking up, I found the moon had risen, and was silvering the mizzen-top and shining white on the luff of the foresail; and almost at the same time the voice of the look-out shouted, 'Land ho!'

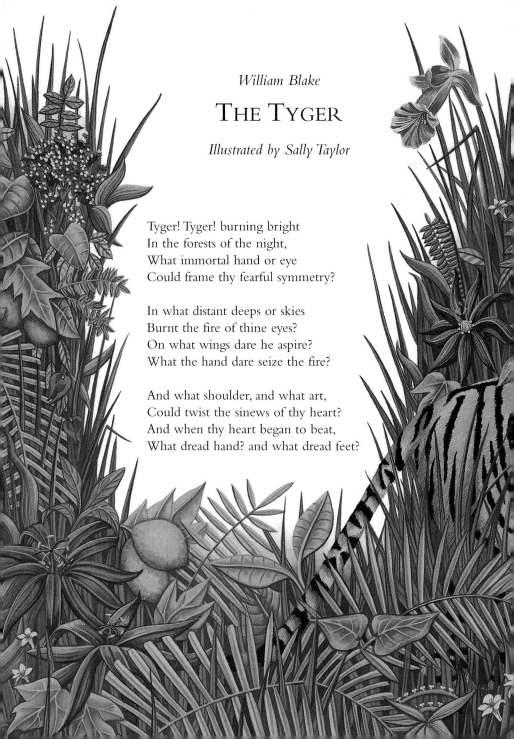

William Blake

THE TYGER

Illustrated by Sally Taylor

Tyger! Tyger! burning bright
In the forests of the night,
What immortal hand or eye
Could frame thy fearful symmetry?

In what distant deeps or skies
Burnt the fire of thine eyes?
On what wings dare he aspire?
What the hand dare seize the fire?

And what shoulder, and what art,
Could twist the sinews of thy heart?
And when thy heart began to beat,
What dread hand? and what dread feet?

What the hammer? what the chain?
In what furnace was thy brain?
What the anvil? what dread grasp
Dare its deadly terrors clasp?

When the stars threw down their spears,
And watered heaven with their tears,
Did he smile his work to see?
Did he who made the Lamb make thee?

Tyger! Tyger! burning bright
In the forests of the night,
What immortal hand or eye,
Dare frame thy fearful symmetry?

Felicia D. Hemans

CASABIANCA

Illustrated by Gino D'Achille

The boy stood on the burning deck,
  Whence all but he had fled;
The flame that lit the battle's wreck
  Shone round him o'er the dead.

Yet beautiful and bright he stood,
  As born to rule the storm;
A creature of heroic blood,
  A proud though childlike form.

The flames rolled on; he would not go
  Without his father's word;
That father, faint in death below,
  His voice no longer heard.

He called aloud, 'Say, Father, say,
  If yet my task be done!'
He knew not that the chieftain lay
  Unconscious of his son.

'Speak, Father!' once again he cried,
  'If I may yet be gone!'
And but the booming shots replied,
  And fast the flames rolled on.

Upon his brow he felt their breath,
  And in his waving hair,
And looked from that lone post of death
  In still yet brave despair;

And shouted but once more aloud,
  'My Father! must I stay?'
While o'er him fast, through sail and shroud,
  The wreathing fires made way.

They wrapped the ship in splendour wild,
  They caught the flag on high,
And streamed above the gallant child,
  Like banners in the sky.

There came a burst of thunder sound;
  The boy – Oh! where was he?
Ask of the winds, that far around
  With fragments strewed the sea –

With mast and helm and pennon fair,
  That well had borne their part –
But the noblest thing that perished there
  Was that young, faithful heart.

Lewis Carroll

YOU ARE OLD, FATHER WILLIAM

Illustrated by Chris Riddell

'You are old, Father William,' the young man said,
  'And your hair has become very white;
And yet you incessantly stand on your head –
  Do you think, at your age, it is right?'

'In my youth,' Father William replied to his son,
  'I feared it might injure the brain;
But, now that I'm perfectly sure I have none,
  Why, I do it again and again.'

'You are old,' said the youth, 'as I mentioned before,
  And have grown most uncommonly fat;
Yet you turned a back-somersault in at the door –
  Pray, what is the reason for that?'

'In my youth,' said the sage, as he shook his grey locks,
  'I kept all my limbs very supple
By the use of this ointment – one shilling the box –
  Allow me to sell you a couple?'

'You are old,' said the youth, 'and your jaws are too weak
  For anything tougher than suet;
Yet you finished the goose, with the bones and the beak –
  Pray, how did you manage to do it?'

'In my youth,' said his father, 'I took to the law,
  And argued each case with my wife;
And the muscular strength, which it gave to my jaw,
  Has lasted the rest of my life.'

'You are old,' said the youth, 'one would hardly suppose
  That your eye was as steady as ever;
Yet you balanced an eel on the end of your nose –
  What made you so awfully clever?'

'I have answered three questions, and that is enough,'
  Said his father. 'Don't give yourself airs!
Do you think I can listen all day to such stuff?
  Be off, or I'll kick you downstairs!'

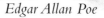

Edgar Allan Poe

ANNABEL LEE

Illustrated by Rosemary Woods

It was many and many a year ago,
  In a kingdom by the sea,
That a maiden there lived whom you may know
  By the name of Annabel Lee;
And this maiden she lived with no other thought
  Than to love and be loved by me.

She was a child and *I* was a child,
  In this kingdom by the sea,
But we loved with a love that was more than love –
  I and my Annabel Lee –
With a love that the wingèd seraphs of Heaven
  Coveted her and me.

And this was the reason that, long ago,
  In this kingdom by the sea,
A wind blew out of a cloud, by night
  Chilling my Annabel Lee;
So that her highborn kinsmen came
  And bore her away from me,
To shut her up in a sepulchre
  In this kingdom by the sea.

The angels, not half so happy in Heaven,
  Went envying her and me: –
Yes! – that was the reason (as all men know,
  In this kingdom by the sea)
That the wind came out of the cloud, chilling
  And killing my Annabel Lee.

But our love it was stronger by far than the love
  Of those who were older than we –
  Of many far wiser than we –
And neither the angels in Heaven above
  Nor the demons down under the sea,
Can ever dissever my soul from the soul
  Of the beautiful Annabel Lee: –

For the moon never beams, without bringing me dreams
  Of the beautiful Annabel Lee;
And the stars never rise but I see the bright eyes
  Of the beautiful Annabel Lee:
And so, all the night-tide, I lie down by the side
Of my darling, my darling, my life and my bride,
  In the sepulchre there by the sea –
  In her tomb by the side of the sea.

Christina Rossetti

WHAT IS PINK?

Illustrated by Ruth Rivers

What is pink? A rose is pink
By the fountain's brink.
What is red? A poppy's red
In its barley bed.
What is blue? The sky is blue
Where the clouds float through.
What is white? A swan is white
Sailing in the light.
What is yellow? Pears are yellow,
Rich and ripe and mellow.
What is green? The grass is green,
With small flowers between.
What is violet? Clouds are violet
In the summer twilight.
What is orange? Why, an orange,
Just an orange!

Carlo Collodi

From

PINOCCHIO

Illustrated by Mauro Evangelista

*Pinocchio, the puppet who wants to be a real boy, meets his
'friends' – the fox and the cat – and goes with them to sow his
money in the Field of Miracles.*

As you may imagine, the
fairy let the puppet scream
and cry a good half hour
because of his long nose which
he could not get through the
door. She did this to teach him a
good lesson, and to correct him of the
very bad habit of lying, which is one of
the worst habits a boy can have. But when
she saw his face disfigured from crying, and his eyes sticking out of
his head, she pitied him. So she clapped her hands, at which signal a
thousand big woodpeckers flew in at the window and, perching on
Pinocchio's nose, pecked away at it with so much zeal that in a few
minutes the big, ridiculous thing was reduced to its usual size.

'How good you are, dear fairy,' said the puppet, wiping his eyes. 'I
love you so much!'

'I love you too,' answered the fairy, 'and if you want to stay with me,
you shall be my little brother, and I will be your darling sister.'

'I'd like to stay with you, but what about my daddy?'

'I have thought of everything, and your father already knows

67

everything. He will be here tonight.'

'Really?' exclaimed Pinocchio, jumping for joy. 'Then, dearest fairy, if you don't mind, I shall go out to meet him. I can't wait any longer to see and kiss that poor old man, who has suffered so much for me!'

'Go, by all means, but don't get lost. Take the road through the wood, and you will surely meet him.'

Pinocchio left; and as soon as he reached the wood he began to run like a deer. At a certain place, in front of the big oak tree, he stopped, because he thought he heard people moving in the bushes. And indeed, there appeared all at once on the road – can you guess who? – the fox and the cat, his two travelling companions, with whom he had supped at the Red Crab Inn.

'Here is our dear Pinocchio,' exclaimed the fox, embracing and kissing him. 'How do you come to be here?'

'How do you come to be here?' repeated the cat.

'It's a very long story,' said the puppet. 'I'll tell it when I have time, though you should know this much – that the other night, when you left me alone in the inn, I encountered assassins on the road.'

'Assassins? Oh, my poor friend Pinocchio! And what did they want?'

'They wanted to rob me of my gold.'

'Infamous people!' said the fox.

'Most infamous people!' added the cat.

'But I ran away,' continued the puppet, 'and they chased me until they caught me, and hung me to a branch of that oak tree.' And Pinocchio pointed to the big oak.

'Did you ever hear anything more horrible!' said the fox. 'What a world we are condemned to live in! Where can honest people like us find shelter?'

While talking, Pinocchio noticed that the cat was lame of her right foreleg, since the paw with all its claws was missing. So he said to her, 'What has become of your paw?'

The cat wanted to say something, but got confused – so the fox answered quickly, 'My friend is too modest. That is why she doesn't answer, but I shall answer for her. About an hour ago we met an old

wolf on the road, who was almost fainting from hunger. He asked alms of us, but we hadn't even a fish bone to give him; so what do you think my friend did – my friend, who has the heart of a Caesar? She bit off her own paw, and gave it to the poor beast, so that he could eat something.' As he told this, the fox wiped a tear.

Pinocchio was so deeply touched that he went to the cat, and whispered in her ear, 'If all cats were like you, mice would be fortunate creatures!'

'And what are you doing here?' asked the fox.

'I'm waiting for my father; he might come any moment.'

'And your gold pieces?'

'They are all in my pocket, except the one I spent at the inn of the Red Crab.'

'And to think that, by tomorrow, instead of four gold pieces they might be a thousand, or two thousand! Why not follow my advice, and bury them in the Field of Miracles?'

'Impossible, today. I'll go another time.'

'Another time will be too late,' said the fox.

'Why?'

'Because a rich man has bought the field, and after tomorrow nobody will be allowed to bury his money there.'

'How far away is the Field of Miracles?'

'Hardly two miles. Will you come with us? You will be there in half an hour, and bury your four gold pieces at once, and after a few minutes you shall have two thousand, and return in the evening with your pockets full. Will you come?'

Pinocchio remembered the good fairy, old Geppetto, and the

warnings of the talking cricket; yet in the end he did as all boys do who have no sense, and no heart – that is, he shook his head and said to the fox and the cat, 'Let's go! I'll come with you.'

And off they went.

They had walked about half a day when they came to a place called Fools' Trap. As soon as they entered the city, Pinocchio saw that the streets were full of dogs who had lost their hair, and whose mouths were wide open from hunger. There were shorn sheep, trembling with cold; roosters without their crests and combs, who were begging for a grain of maize; butterflies who could not fly, because they had sold their beautiful wings; peacocks without tails, who were ashamed to be seen; and pheasants who were crawling along, mourning for their beautiful gold and silver feathers, lost for ever.

In the midst of these beggars and shame-faced beasts, from time to time elegant carriages passed by, with a fox, or a thievish magpie, or some bird of prey inside.

'But where is the Field of Miracles?' asked Pinocchio.

'Just a few yards from here.'

They crossed the city and, going beyond the walls, they came to a lonely field that looked just like any other field.

'Here we are,' said the fox. 'Now, get to work and dig a small hole with your hands and put your gold pieces in.'

Pinocchio obeyed. He dug a hole, put into it the four gold pieces he still had, and covered them up with some earth.

'Now, then,' said the fox, 'go to the dam close by, bring a bucket of water, and water the ground where you have sown your fortune.'

Pinocchio went to the dam and, as he did not have a

bucket, he took one of his old shoes, filled it with water, and watered the earth which covered his money.

'What else must I do?'

'Nothing else,' answered the fox. 'Now we can go away. You must come back in about twenty minutes, and you will see a little tree already growing through the earth, with its branches covered with money.'

The poor puppet was beside himself with joy, and he thanked the fox and the cat a thousand times, and promised them a lovely present.

'We don't want presents,' answered those two scoundrels. 'It's quite enough for us to have shown you how to get rich without hard work. That makes us as happy as can be.'

With these words they said good-bye to Pinocchio and, wishing him a splendid harvest, they went about their business.

William Blake

AUGURIES OF INNOCENCE

Illustrated by Siân Bailey

To see a World in a Grain of Sand
And a Heaven in a Wild Flower,
Hold Infinity in the palm of your hand
And Eternity in an hour.

Mary Howitt

THE SPIDER AND THE FLY

Illustrated by Fritz Wegner

'Will you walk into my parlour?' said the Spider to the Fly,
''Tis the prettiest little parlour that ever you did spy;
The way into my parlour is up a winding stair,
And I have many curious things to show when you are there.'
'Oh no, no,' said the little Fly, 'to ask me is in vain,
For who goes up your winding stair can ne'er come down again.'

sweet
Creature!

'I'm sure you must be weary, dear, with soaring up so high;
Will you rest upon my little bed?' said the Spider to the Fly.
'There are pretty curtains drawn around, the sheets are fine and thin;
And if you like to rest awhile, I'll snugly tuck you in!'
'Oh no, no,' said the little Fly, 'for I've often heard it said,
They never, never wake again, who sleep upon your bed!'

Said the cunning Spider to the Fly, 'Dear friend, what can I do,
To prove the warm affection I've always felt for you?
I have within my pantry good store of all that's nice;
I'm sure you're very welcome – will you please to take a slice?'
'Oh no, no,' said the little Fly, 'kind sir, that cannot be,
I've heard what's in your pantry, and I do not wish to see.'

'Sweet creature,' said the Spider, 'you're witty and you're wise;
How handsome are your gauzy wings, how brilliant are your eyes!
I have a little looking-glass upon my parlour shelf,
If you'll step in a moment, dear, you shall behold yourself.'
'I thank you, gentle sir,' she said, 'for what you're pleased to say,
And bidding you good morning now, I'll call another day.'

The Spider turned him round about, and went into his den,
For well he knew the silly Fly would soon come back again;
So he wove a subtle web, in a little corner sly,
And set his table ready, to dine upon the Fly.
Then he came out to his door again, and merrily did sing:
'Come hither, hither, pretty Fly, with the pearl and silver wing;
Your robes are green and purple – there's a crest upon your head;
Your eyes are like the diamond bright, but mine are dull as lead.'

Alas, alas! how very soon this silly little Fly,
Hearing his wily, flattering words, came slowly flitting by;
With buzzing wings she hung aloft, then near and nearer drew,
Thinking only of her brilliant eyes, and green and purple hue;
Thinking only of her crested head – poor foolish thing! At last,
Up jumped the cunning Spider, and fiercely held her fast.
He dragged her up his winding stair, into his dismal den,
Within his little parlour – but she ne'er came out again!

Lady Lindsay

DAY AND NIGHT

Illustrated by Alison Jay

Said Day to Night,
'I bring God's light.
 What gift have you?'
 Night said, 'The dew.'

'I give bright hours,'
Quoth Day, 'and flowers.'
 Said Night, 'More blest,
 I bring sweet rest.'

Mark Twain

THE ADVENTURES OF HUCKLEBERRY FINN

Illustrated by Richard Jones

Having feigned his own death to escape his brutal father,
Huckleberry Finn sets out on a journey to start a new life.
On the way he meets up with an old friend.

I was pretty hungry, but it warn't going to do for me to start a fire, because they might see the smoke. So I set there and watched the cannon-smoke and listened to the boom. The river was a mile wide, there, and it always looks pretty on a summer morning – so I was having a good enough time seeing them hunt for my remainders, if I only had a bite to eat. Well, then I happened to think how they always put quicksilver in loaves of bread and float them off because they always go right to the drownded carcass and stop there. So says I, I'll keep a look-out, and if any of them's floating around after me, I'll give them a show. I changed to the Illinois edge of the island to see what luck I could have, and I warn't disappointed. A big double loaf come along, and I most got it, with a long stick, but my foot slipped and she floated out further. Of course I was where the current set in the closest to the shore – I knowed enough for that. But by-and-by along comes another one, and this time I won. I took out the plug and shook out the little

dab of quicksilver, and set my teeth in.
It was 'baker's bread' – what the quality eat
– none of your low-down cornpone.

I got a good place amongst the leaves, and set
there on a log, munching the bread and watching
the ferry-boat, and very well satisfied. And then
something struck me. I says, now I reckon the widow
or the parson or somebody prayed that this bread would
find me, and here it has gone and done it. So there ain't
no doubt but there is something in that thing. That is,
there's something in it when a body like the widow or the parson
prays, but it don't work for me, and I reckon it don't work for only just
the right kind.

I lit a pipe and had a good long smoke and went on watching. The
ferry-boat was floating with the current, and I allowed I'd have a
chance to see who was aboard when she come along, because she
would come in close, where the bread did. When she'd got pretty well
along down towards me, I put out my pipe and went to where I fished
out the bread, and laid down behind a log on the bank in a little open
place. Where the log forked I could peep through.

By-and-by she come along, and she drifted in so close that they
could a run out a plank and walked ashore. Most everybody was on
the boat. Pap, and Judge Thatcher, and Bessie Thatcher, and Jo Harper,
and Tom Sawyer, and his old Aunt Polly, and Sid and Mary, and
plenty more. Everybody was talking about the murder, but the captain
broke in and says:

'Look sharp, now; the current sets in the closest here, and maybe he's
washed ashore and got tangled amongst the brush at the water's edge.
I hope so, anyway.'

I didn't hope so. They all crowded up and leaned over the rails,
nearly in my face, and kept still, watching with all their might. I could
see them first-rate, but they couldn't see me. Then the captain sung
out:

'Stand away!' and the cannon let off such a blast right before me that it made me deaf with the noise and pretty near blind with the smoke, and I judged I was gone. If they'd a had some bullets in, I reckon they'd a got the corpse they was after. Well, I see I warn't hurt, thanks to goodness. The boat floated on and went out of sight around the shoulder of the island. I could hear the booming, now and then, further and further off, and by-and-by after an hour, I didn't hear it no more. The island was three mile long. I judged they had got to the foot, and was giving it up But they didn't yet awhile. They turned around the foot of the island and started up the channel on the Missouri side, under steam, and booming once in a while as they went. I crossed over to that side and watched them. When they got abreast the head of the island they quit shooting and dropped over to the Missouri shore and went home to the town.

I knowed I was all right now. Nobody else would come a-hunting after me. I got my traps out of the canoe and made me a nice camp in the thick woods. I made a kind of a tent out of my blankets to put my things under so the rain couldn't get at them. I catched a cat-fish and haggled him open with my saw, and towards sundown I started my camp-fire and had supper. Then I set out a line to catch some fish for breakfast.

When it was dark I set by my camp-fire smoking, and feeling pretty satisfied; but by-and-by it got sort of lonesome, and so I went and set on the bank and listened to the currents washing along, and counted the stars and drift-logs and rafts that come down, and then went to bed; there ain't no better way to put in time when you are lonesome; you can't stay so, you soon get over it.

And so for three days and nights. No difference – just the same thing. But the next day I went exploring around down through the island. I was boss of it; it all belonged to me, so to say, and I wanted to know all about it; but mainly I wanted to put in the time. I found plenty strawberries, ripe and prime; and green summer-grapes, and green razberries; and the green blackberries was just beginning to show. They would all come handy by-and-by, I judged.

Well, I went fooling along in the deep woods till I judged I warn't

far from the foot of the island. I had my gun along, but I hadn't shot nothing; it was for protection; thought I would kill some game nigh home. About this time I mighty near stepped on a good-sized snake, and it went sliding off through the grass and flowers, and I after it, trying to get a shot at it. I clipped along, and all of a sudden I bounded right on to the ashes of a camp-fire that was still smoking.

My heart jumped up amongst my lungs. I never waited for to look further, but uncocked my gun and went sneaking back on my tip-toes as fast as ever I could. Every now and then I stopped a second, amongst the thick leaves, and listened; but my breath come so hard I couldn't hear nothing else. I slunk along another piece further, then listened again; and so on, and so on; if I see a stump, I took it for a man; if I trod on a stick and broke it, it made me feel like a person had cut one of my breaths in two and I only got half, and the short half, too.

When I got to camp I warn't feeling very brash, there warn't much sand in my craw; but I says, this ain't no time to be fooling around. So I got all my traps into my canoe again so as to have them out of sight, and I put out the fire and scattered the ashes around to look like an old last year's camp, and then clumb a tree.

I reckon I was up in the tree two hours; but I didn't see nothing, I didn't hear nothing – I only thought I heard and seen as much as a thousand things. Well, I couldn't stay up there for ever; so at last I got down, but I kept in the thick woods and on the look-out all the time. All I could get to eat was berries and what was left over from breakfast.

By the time it was night I was pretty hungry. So when it was good and dark, I slid out from shore before moonrise and paddled over to the Illinois bank – about a quarter of a mile. I went out in the woods and cooked a supper, and I had about made up my mind I would stay there all night, when I hear a *plunkety-plunk, plunkety-plunk*, and says to myself, horses coming; and next I hear people's voices. I got everything into the canoe as quick as I could, and then went creeping through the woods to see what I could find out. I hadn't got far when I hear a man say:

'We better camp here, if we can find a good place; the horses is about beat out. Let's look around.'

I didn't wait, but shoved out and paddled away easy. I tied up in the old place, and reckoned I would sleep in the canoe.

I didn't sleep much. I couldn't, somehow, for thinking. And every time I waked up I thought somebody had me by the neck. So the sleep didn't do me no good. By-and-by I says to myself, I can't live this way; I'm agoing to find out who it is that's here on the island with me; I'll find it out or bust. Well, I felt better, right off.

So I took my paddle and slid out from shore just a step or two, and then let the canoe drop along down amongst the shadows. The moon was shining, and outside of the shadows it made it most as light as day. I poked along well on to an hour, everything still as rocks and sound asleep. Well, by this time I was most down to the foot of the island. A little ripply, cool breeze begun to blow, and that was as good as saying the night was about done. I give her a turn with the paddle and brung her nose to shore; then I got my gun and slipped out and into the edge of the woods. I set down there on a log and looked out through the leaves. I see the moon go off watch and the darkness begin to blanket the river. But in a little while I see a pale streak over the tree-tops, and knowed the day was coming. So I took my gun and slipped off towards where I had run across that camp-fire, stopping every minute or two to listen. But I hadn't no luck, somehow; I couldn't seem to find the place. But by-and-by, sure enough, I catched a glimpse of fire, away through the trees. I went for it, cautious and slow. By-and-by I was close enough to have a look, and there laid a man on the ground. It most give me the fan-tods. He had a blanket around his head, and his head was nearly in the fire. I set there behind a clump of bushes, in about six foot of him, and kept my eyes on him steady. It was getting grey daylight, now. Pretty soon he gapped, and stretched himself, and hove off the blanket, and it was Miss Watson's Jim! I bet I was glad to see him. I says:

'Hello, Jim!' and skipped out.

He bounced up and stared at me wild. Then he drops down on his knees, and puts his hands together and says:

'Doan' hurt me – don't! I hain't ever done no harm to a ghos'. I awluz liked dead people, en done all I could for 'em. You go en git in de river agin, whah you b'longs, en doan' do nuffin' to Ole Jim, 'at 'uz awluz yo' fren'.'

Well, I warn't long making him understand I warn't dead. I was ever so glad to see Jim. I warn't lonesome, now. I told him I warn't afraid of *him* telling the people where I was. I talked along, but he only set there and looked at me; never said nothing. Then I says:

'It's good daylight. Le's get breakfast. Make up your camp-fire good.'

'What's de use er makin' up de camp-fire to cook strawbries en sich truck? But you got a gun, hain't you? Den we kin git sumfin' better den strawbries.'

'Strawberries and such truck,' I says. 'Is that what you live on?'

'I couldn' git nuffin' else,' he says.

'Why, how long you been on the island, Jim?'

'I come heah de night arter you's killed.'

'What, all that time?'

'Yes-indeedy.'

'And ain't you had nothing but that kind of rubbage to eat?'

'No, sah – nuffin' else.'

'Well, you must be most starved, ain't you?'

'I reck'n I could eat a hoss. I think I could. How long you ben on de islan'?'

'Since the night I got killed.'

'No! W'y, what has you lived on? But you got a gun? Oh, yes, you got a gun. Dat's good. Now you kill sumfn' en I'll make up de fire.'

So we went over to where the canoe was, and while he built a fire in a grassy open place amongst the trees, I fetched meal and bacon and coffee, and coffee-pot and frying-pan, and sugar and tin cups, and the

nigger was set back considerable, because he reckoned it was all done with witchcraft. I catched a good big cat-fish, too, and Jim cleaned him with his knife, and fried him.

When breakfast was ready, we lolled on the grass and eat it smoking hot; Jim laid it in with all his might, for he was most about starved. Then when we had got pretty well stuffed, we laid off and lazied.

By-and-by Jim says:

'But looky here, Huck, who wuz it dat 'uz killed in dat shanty, ef it warn't you?'

Then I told him the whole thing, and he said it was smart. He said Tom Sawyer couldn't get up no better plan than what I had. Then I says:

'How do you come to be here, Jim, and how'd you get here?'

He looked pretty uneasy, and didn't say nothing for a minute. Then he says:

'Maybe I better not tell.'

'Why, Jim?'

'Well, dey's reasons. But you wouldn't tell on me ef I 'uz to tell you, would you, Huck?'

'Blamed if I would, Jim.'

'Well, I b'lieve you, Huck. I – I run *off.*'

'Jim!'

'But mind, you said you wouldn't tell – you know you said you wouldn't tell, Huck.'

'Well, I did. I said I wouldn't, and I'll stick to it. Honest *injun* I will. People would call me a low-down Ablitionist and despise me for keeping mum – but that don't make no difference. I ain't agoing to tell, and I ain't agoing back there anyways. So now, le's know all about it.'

Alfred, Lord Tennyson

THE EAGLE

Illustrated by Sue Williams

He clasps the crag with crooked hands;
Close to the sun in lonely lands,
Ringed with the azure world, he stands.

The wrinkled sea beneath him crawls;
He watches from his mountain walls,
And like a thunderbolt he falls.

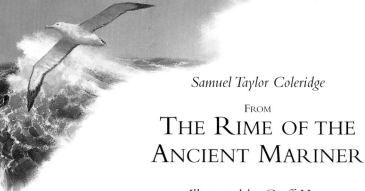

Samuel Taylor Coleridge

FROM

THE RIME OF THE
ANCIENT MARINER

Illustrated by Geoff Hunt

The ancient Mariner tells of his fateful deed.

'And now there came both mist and snow,
And it grew wondrous cold:
And ice, mast-high, came floating by,
As green as emerald.

And through the drifts the snowy clifts
Did send a dismal sheen:
Nor shapes of men nor beasts we ken –
The ice was all between.

The ice was here, the ice was there,
The ice was all around:
It cracked and growled, and roared and howled,
Like noises in a swound!

At length did cross an Albatross,
Through the fog it came;
As if it had been a Christian soul,
We hailed it in God's name.

It ate the food it ne'er had eat,
And round and round it flew.
The ice did split with a thunder-fit;
 The helmsman steered us through!

And a good south wind sprung up behind;
The Albatross did follow,
And every day, for food or play,
Came to the mariner's hollo!

In mist or cloud, on mast or shroud,
It perched for vespers nine;
Whiles all the night, through fog-smoke white,
Glimmered the white Moon-shine.'

'God save thee, ancient Mariner!
From the fiends, that plague thee thus! –
Why look'st thou so?' – 'With my cross-bow
I shot the ALBATROSS.'

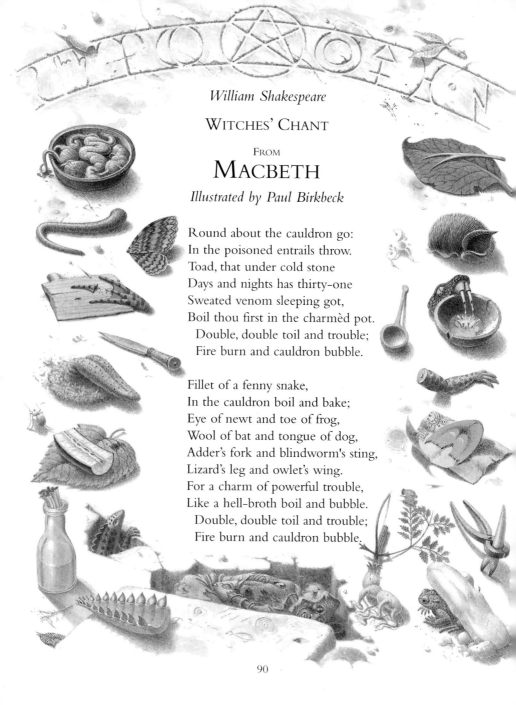

William Shakespeare

WITCHES' CHANT

FROM

MACBETH

Illustrated by Paul Birkbeck

Round about the cauldron go:
In the poisoned entrails throw.
Toad, that under cold stone
Days and nights has thirty-one
Sweated venom sleeping got,
Boil thou first in the charmèd pot.
   Double, double toil and trouble;
   Fire burn and cauldron bubble.

Fillet of a fenny snake,
In the cauldron boil and bake;
Eye of newt and toe of frog,
Wool of bat and tongue of dog,
Adder's fork and blindworm's sting,
Lizard's leg and owlet's wing.
For a charm of powerful trouble,
Like a hell-broth boil and bubble.
   Double, double toil and trouble;
   Fire burn and cauldron bubble.

Scale of dragon, tooth of wolf,
Witch's mummy, maw and gulf
Of the ravenous salt-sea shark,
Root of hemlock digged in the dark,
Make the gruel thick and slab:
Add thereto a tiger's chaudron,
For the ingredients of our cauldron.
  Double, double toil and trouble,
  Fire burn and cauldron bubble.

As Good as His Word

FROM

Aesop's Fables

Illustrated by James Marsh

Aesop was a storyteller in the sixth century BC. His animal fables have survived the centuries, and many are so well known they have given us phrases we use every day.

A mouse ran over the body of a sleeping lion. Waking up, the lion seized it and was minded to eat it. But when the mouse begged to be released, promising to repay him if he would spare it, he laughed and let it go. Not long afterwards its gratitude was the means of saving his life. Being captured by hunters, he was tied by a rope to a tree. The mouse heard his groans, and running to the spot freed him by gnawing through the rope. 'You laughed at me the other day,' it said, 'because you did not expect me to repay your kindness. Now you see that even mice are grateful.'

A change of fortune can make the strongest person need a weaker person's help.

Daniel Defoe

ROBINSON CRUSOE

Illustrated by Adrian Chesterman

The sole survivor of a shipwreck, Robinson Crusoe has no human contact for over twenty-five years – until one Friday he rescues a prisoner.

About a year and a half after I had entertained these notions, I was surprised one morning early, with seeing no less than five canoes all on shore together on my side of the island; and the people who belonged to them all landed, and out of my sight. The number of them broke all my measures, for seeing so many, and knowing that they always came four or six, or sometimes more in a boat, I could not tell what to think of it, or how to attack twenty or thirty men single-handed; so I lay still in my castle, perplexed and discomforted; however, I put myself into all the same postures for an attack that I had formerly provided, and was just ready for action, if anything had presented. Having waited a good while, listening to hear if they made any noise, at length, being very impatient, I set my guns at the foot of my ladder, and clambered up to the top of the hill; standing so, however, that my head did not appear above the hill, so that they could not perceive me by any means; here I observed, by the help of my perspective-glass, that they were no less

94

than thirty in number, that they had a
fire kindled, that they had had meat
dressed. How they cooked it, that I knew
not, or what it was; but they were all
dancing in I know not how many
barbarous gestures and figures, their
own way, round the fire.

While I was thus looking on
them, I perceived two miserable
wretches dragged from the boats,
where it seems they were laid by,
and were now brought out for
the slaughter. I perceived one of
them immediately fall, being
knocked down, I suppose with a club
or wooden sword, for that was their
way, and two or three others were at work
immediately cutting him open for their
cookery, while the other victim was left standing by himself, till
they should be ready for him. In that very moment this poor wretch
seeing himself a little at liberty, nature inspired him with hopes of life,
and he started away from them, and ran with incredible swiftness along
the sands directly towards me, I mean towards that part of the coast
where my habitation was.

I was dreadfully frightened (that I must acknowledge) when I
perceived him to run my way, and especially when, as I thought, I saw
him pursued by the whole body; and now I expected that part of my
dream was coming to pass, and that he would certainly take shelter in
my grove; but I could not depend by any means upon my dream for
the rest of it – that the other savages would not pursue him thither,
and find him there. However, I kept my station, and my spirits began
to recover when I found that only three men followed him, and still
more was I encouraged when I found that he outstripped them
exceedingly in running, and gained ground of them, so that if he could

but hold it for half an hour, I saw easily he would fairly get away from them all.

There was between them and my castle the creek which I mentioned at the first part of my story; and this, I saw plainly, he must necessarily swim over, or the poor wretch would be taken there. But when the savage escaping came thither, he made nothing of it, though the tide was then up, but plunging in, swam through in about thirty strokes or thereabouts, landed, and ran on with exceeding strength and swiftness; when the three persons came to the creek, I found that two of them could swim, but the third could not, and that standing on the other side, he looked at the other, but went no further, and soon after went softly back again, which, as it happened, was very well for him in the main.

I observed that the two who swam were yet more than twice as long swimming over the creek as the fellow was that fled from them. It came now very warmly upon my thought, and indeed irresistibly, that now was my time to get me a servant, and perhaps a companion or assistant; and that I was called plainly by Providence to save this poor creature's life; I immediately ran down the ladders with all possible expedition, fetched my two guns, for they were both but at the foot of the ladders, as I observed above; and getting up again, with the same haste, to the top of the hill, I crossed toward the sea; and having a very short cut, and all downhill, thrust myself in the way between the pursuers and the pursued; shouting aloud to him that fled, who looking back, was at first·perhaps as much frightened at me as at them; but I beckoned with my hand to him to come back; and in the meantime, I slowly advanced towards the two that followed; then rushing at once upon the foremost, I knocked him down with the stock of my piece; I was loath to fire, because I would not have the rest hear; though at that distance it would not have been easily heard, and being out of sight of the smoke too, they would not have easily known what to make of it. Having knocked this fellow down, the other who pursued with him stopped, as if he had been frighted; and I advanced apace towards him; but as I came nearer, I perceived he had a bow and

arrow, and was fitting it to shoot at me; so I was then necessitated to shoot at him first, which I did, and killed him at the first shot; the poor savage who fled, but had stopped, though he saw both his enemies fallen and killed, as he thought, yet was so frightened with the fire and noise of my piece, that he stood stock still, and neither came forward or went backward, though he seemed rather inclined to fly still than to come on; I called again to him, and made signs to come forward, which he easily understood, and came a little way, then stopped again, and then a little further, and stopped again, and I could then perceive that he stood trembling, as if he had been taken prisoner, and had just been to be killed, as his two enemies were. I beckoned him again to come to me, and gave him all the signs of encouragement that I could think of, and he came nearer and nearer, kneeling down every ten or twelve steps in token of acknowledgement for my saving his life. I smiled at him, and looked pleasantly, and beckoned to him to come still nearer; at length he came close to me, and then he kneeled down again, kissed the ground, and laid his head upon the ground, and taking me by the foot, set my foot upon his head; this it seems was in token of swearing to be my slave for ever; I took him up, and made much of him, and encouraged him all I could. But there was more work to do yet, for I perceived the savage who I knocked down was not killed, but stunned with the blow, and began to come to himself; so I pointed to him, and showing him the savage, that he was not dead; upon this he spoke some words to me, and though I could not understand them, yet I thought they were pleasant to hear, for they were the first sound of a man's voice that I had heard, my own excepted, for above twenty-five years. But there was no time for such reflections now; the savage who was knocked down recovered himself so far as to sit up upon the ground, and I perceived that my savage began to be afraid; but when I saw that, I presented my other piece at the man, as if I would shoot him; upon this my savage, for so I call him now, made a motion to me to lend him my sword, which hung naked in a belt by my side; so I did: he no sooner had it, but he runs to his enemy, and at one blow cut off his head as cleverly, no executioner could have done it sooner or better; which I thought very strange, for one who I had reason to believe never saw a sword in his life before, except their own wooden swords; however, it seems, as I learned afterwards, they make their wooden swords so sharp, so heavy, and the wood is so hard, that they will cut off heads even with them, ay and arms, and that at one blow too; when he had done this, he comes laughing to me in sign of triumph, and brought me the sword again, and with abundance of gestures which I did not understand, laid it down with the head of the savage that he had killed, just before me.

But that which astonished him most, was to know how I had killed the other Indian so far off; so pointing to him, he made signs to me to let him go to him, so I bade him go, as well as I could; when he came to him, he stood like one amazed, looking at him, turned him first on one side, then on t'other, looked at the wound the bullet had made, which it seems was just in his breast, where it had made a hole, and no great quantity of blood had followed, but he had bled inwardly, for he was quite dead. He took up his bow and arrows, and came back, so I turned to go away, and beckoned to him to follow me, making signs to him that more might come after him.

Upon this he signed to me that he should bury them with sand, that they might not be seen by the rest if they followed; and so I made signs again to him to do so; he fell to work, and in an instant he had scraped a hole in the sand with his hands, big enough to bury the first in, and then dragged him into it, and covered him, and did so also by the other; I believe he had buried them both in a quarter of an hour; then calling him away, I took him not to my castle, but quite away to my cave, on the farther part of the island; so I did not let my dream come to pass in that part, that he came into my grove for shelter.

Here I gave him bread, and a bunch of raisins to eat, and a draught of water, which I found he was indeed in great distress for, by his running; and having refreshed him, I made signs for him to go lie down and sleep; pointing to a place where I had laid a great parcel of rice straw, and a blanket upon it, which I used to sleep upon myself sometimes; so the poor creature laid down, and went to sleep.

He was a comely handsome fellow, perfectly well made; with straight, strong limbs, not too large; tall and well shaped, and, as I reckon, about twenty-six years of age. He had a very good countenance, not a fierce and surly aspect; his hair was long and black, not curled like wool; his forehead very high and large, and a great vivacity and sparkling sharpness in his eyes. The colour of his skin was not quite

black, but very tawny; his face was round and plump; his nose small, not flat like the negroes, a very good mouth, thin lips, and his fine teeth well set, and white as ivory. After he had slumbered, rather than slept, about half an hour, he waked again, and comes out of the cave to me; for I had been milking the goats, which I had in the enclosure just by; when he espied me, he came running to me, laying himself down again upon the ground, with all the possible signs of an humble thankful disposition, making many gestures to show it. At last he lays his head flat upon the ground, close to my foot, and sets my other foot upon his head, as he had done before; and after this, made all the signs to me of subjection, servitude, and submission imaginable, to let me know how he would serve me as long as he lived. I understood him in many things, and let him know I was very well pleased with him; in a little time I began to speak to him, and teach him to speak to me; and first, I made him know his name should be Friday, which was the day I saved his life.

Henry Wadsworth Longfellow

HIAWATHA'S CHILDHOOD

FROM

THE SONG OF HIAWATHA

Illustrated by Sue Williams

Then the little Hiawatha
Learned of every bird its language,
Learned their names and all their secrets:
How they built their nests in Summer,
Where they hid themselves in Winter,
Talked with them whene'er he met them,
Called them 'Hiawatha's Chickens'.

Of all the beasts he learned the language,
Learned their names and all their secrets,
How the beavers built their lodges,
How the squirrels hid their acorns,
How the reindeer ran so swiftly,
Why the rabbit was so timid;
Talked with them whene'er he met them,
Called them 'Hiawatha's Brothers'.

Then Iagoo, the great boaster,
He the marvellous story-teller,
He the traveller and the talker,
He the friend of old Nokomis,
Made a bow for Hiawatha:
From a branch of ash he made it,
From an oak-bough made the arrows,
Tipped with flint, and winged with feathers,
And the cord he made of deer-skin.

Then he said to Hiawatha:
'Go, my son, into the forest,
Where the red deer herd together,
Kill for us a famous roebuck,
Kill for us a deer with antlers!'

Forth into the forest straightway
All alone walked Hiawatha
Proudly, with his bows and arrows;
And the birds sang round him, o'er him,
'Do not shoot us, Hiawatha!'
Sang the robin, the Opechee,
Sang the bluebird, the Owaissa,
'Do not shoot us, Hiawatha!'

Up the oak-tree, close beside him,
Sprang the squirrel, Adjidaumo,
In and out among the branches,
Coughed and chattered from the oak-tree,
Laughed, and said between his laughing,
'Do not shoot me, Hiawatha!'

And the rabbit from his pathway
Leaped aside, and at a distance
Sat erect upon his haunches,
Half in fear and half in frolic,
Saying to the little hunter,
'Do not shoot me, Hiawatha!'

But he heeded not, nor heard them,
For his thoughts were with the red deer;
On their tracks his eyes were fastened,
Leading downward to the river,
To the ford across the river,
And as one in slumber walked he.

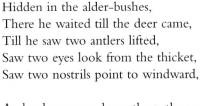

Hidden in the alder-bushes,
There he waited till the deer came,
Till he saw two antlers lifted,
Saw two eyes look from the thicket,
Saw two nostrils point to windward,

And a deer came down the pathway,
Flecked with leafy light and shadow;
And his heart within him fluttered,
Trembled like the leaves above him,
Like the birch-leaf palpitated,
As the deer came down the pathway.

Then, upon one knee uprising,
Hiawatha aimed an arrow;
Scarce a twig moved with his motion,
Scarce a leaf was stirred or rustled,
But the wary roebuck started,
Stamped with all his hoofs together,
Listened with one foot uplifted,
Leaped as if to meet the arrow;
Ah the singing, fatal arrow,
Like a wasp it buzzed and stung him.

Dead he lay there in the forest
By the ford across the river;
Beat his timid heart no longer;
But the heart of Hiawatha
Throbbed and shouted and exulted,
As he bore the red deer homeward;
But Iagoo and Nokomis
Hailed his coming with applauses.

From the red deer's hide, Nokomis
Made a cloak for Hiawatha;
From the deer's flesh Nokomis
Made a banquet in his honour.
All the village came and feasted,
All the guests praised Hiawatha,
Called him Strong-Heart, Soan-getaha!
Called him Loon-heart, Mahn-go-taysee!

Robert Louis Stevenson

FROM A RAILWAY CARRIAGE

Illustrated by Ian Beck

Faster than fairies, faster than witches,
Bridges and houses, hedges and ditches;
And charging along like troops in a battle,
All through the meadows the horses and cattle:
All of the sights of the hill and the plain
Fly as thick as driving rain;
And ever again, in the wink of an eye,
Painted stations whistle by.

Here is a child who clambers and scrambles,
All by himself and gathering brambles;
Here is a tramp who stands and gazes;
And there is the green for stringing the daisies!
Here is a cart run away in the road
Lumping along with man and load;
And here is a mill, and there is a river:
Each a glimpse and gone for ever!

Edward Lear

THE JUMBLIES

Illustrated by Paul Birkbeck

I

They went to sea in a Sieve, they did,
  In a Sieve they went to sea:
In spite of all their friends could say,
On a winter's morn, on a stormy day,
  In a Sieve they went to sea!
And when the Sieve turned round and round,
And every one cried, 'You'll all be drowned!'
They called aloud, 'Our Sieve ain't big,
But we don't care a button! we don't care a fig!
  In a Sieve we'll go to sea!'
    Far and few, far and few,
      Are the lands where the Jumblies live;
      Their heads are green, and their hands are blue,
        And they went to sea in a Sieve.

II

They sailed away in a Sieve, they did,
　In a Sieve they sailed so fast,
With only a beautiful pea-green veil
Tied with a riband by way of a sail,
　To a small tobacco-pipe mast;
And every one said, who saw them go,
'O won't they be soon upset, you know!
For the sky is dark, and the voyage is long,
And happen what may, it's extremely wrong
　In a Sieve to sail so fast!'
　　Far and few, far and few,
　　　Are the lands where the Jumblies live;
　　　Their heads are green, and their hands are blue,
　　　And they went to sea in a Sieve.

III

The water it soon came in, it did,
　The water it soon came in;
So to keep them dry, they wrapped their feet
In a pinky paper all folded neat,
　And they fastened it down with a pin.
And they passed the night in a crockery-jar,
And each of them said, 'How wise we are!
Though the sky be dark, and the voyage be long,
Yet we never can think we were rash or wrong,
　While round in our Sieve we spin!'
　　Far and few, far and few,
　　　Are the lands where the Jumblies live;
　　　Their heads are green, and their hands are blue,
　　　And they went to sea in a Sieve.

IV

And all night long they sailed away;
  And when the sun went down,
They whistled and warbled a moony song
To the echoing sound of a coppery gong,
  In the shade of the mountains brown.
'O Timballo! How happy we are,
When we live in a Sieve and a crockery-jar,
And all night long in the moonlight pale,
We sail away with a pea–green sail,
  In the shade of the mountains brown!'
    Far and few, far and few,
      Are the lands where the Jumblies live;
      Their heads are green, and their hands are blue,
      And they went to sea in a Sieve.

Clement Clarke Moore

A VISIT FROM ST NICHOLAS

Illustrated by Alison Jay

'Twas the night before Christmas, when all through the house
Not a creature was stirring, not even a mouse;
The stockings were hung by the chimney with care,
In hopes that St Nicholas soon would be there;
The children were nestled all snug in their beds,
While visions of sugar-plums danced in their heads;
And Mamma in her kerchief, and I in my cap,
Had just-settled our brains for a long winter's nap –
When out on the lawn there arose such a clatter,
I sprang from my bed to see what was the matter.
Away to the window I flew like a flash,
Tore open the shutters and threw up the sash.
The moon, on the breast of the new-fallen snow,
Gave a lustre of mid-day to objects below;
When, what to my wondering eyes should appear,
But a miniature sleigh, and eight tiny reindeer,
With a little old driver, so lively and quick,
I knew in a moment it must be St Nick.
More rapid than eagles his coursers they came,
And he whistled, and shouted, and called them by name;
'Now, Dasher! now, Dancer! now, Prancer and Vixen!
On! Comet, on! Cupid, on! Donder and Blitzen –
To the top of the porch, to the top of the wall!
Now, dash away, dash away, dash away all!'
As dry leaves that before the wild hurricane fly,

When they meet with an obstacle, mount to the sky,
So, up to the house-top the coursers they flew,
With the sleigh full of toys – and St Nicholas too.
And then in a twinkling I heard on the roof
The prancing and pawing of each little hoof.
As I drew in my head, and was turning around,

Down the chimney St Nicholas came with a bound.
He was dressed all in fur from his head to his foot,
And his clothes were all tarnished with ashes and soot;
A bundle of toys he had flung on his back,
And he looked like a pedlar just opening his pack.
His eyes how they twinkled! his dimples how merry!
His cheeks were like roses, his nose like a cherry;
His droll little mouth was drawn up like a bow,
And the beard on his chin was as white as the snow.
The stump of a pipe he held tight in his teeth,
And the smoke, it encircled his head like a wreath.
He had a broad face and a little round belly
That shook, when he laughed, like a bowl full of jelly.
He was chubby and plump – a right jolly old elf;
And I laughed when I saw him, in spite of myself.
A wink of his eye, and a twist of his head,
Soon gave me to know I had nothing to dread.
He spoke not a word, but went straight to his work,
And filled all the stockings; then turned with a jerk,
And laying his finger aside of his nose,
And giving a nod, up the chimney he rose.
He sprang to his sleigh, to his team gave a whistle,
And away they all flew like the down of a thistle;
But I heard him exclaim, ere he drove out of sight,
'Happy Christmas to all, and to all a good-night!'

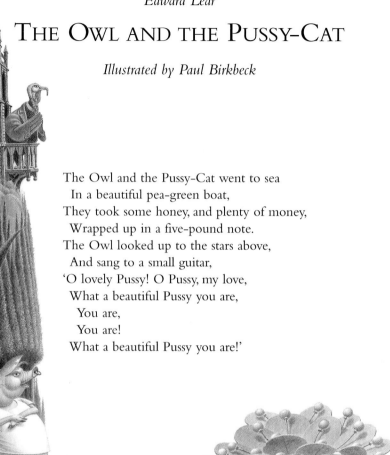

Edward Lear

THE OWL AND THE PUSSY-CAT

Illustrated by Paul Birkbeck

The Owl and the Pussy-Cat went to sea
  In a beautiful pea-green boat,
They took some honey, and plenty of money,
  Wrapped up in a five-pound note.
The Owl looked up to the stars above,
  And sang to a small guitar,
'O lovely Pussy! O Pussy, my love,
  What a beautiful Pussy you are,
    You are,
    You are!
  What a beautiful Pussy you are!'

Pussy said to the Owl, 'You elegant fowl!
  How charmingly sweet you sing!
O let us be married! too long we have tarried
  But what shall we do for a ring?'
They sailed away for a year and a day,
  To the land where the Bong-tree grows,
And there in a wood a Piggy-wig stood,
  With a ring at the end of his nose,
    His nose,
    His nose,
  With a ring at the end of his nose.

'Dear Pig, are you willing to sell for one shilling
  Your ring?' Said the Piggy, 'I will.'
So they took it away, and were married next day
  By the Turkey who lives on the hill.
They dined on mince, and slices of quince,
  Which they ate with a runcible spoon;
And hand in hand, on the edge of the sand,
  They danced by the light of the moon,
    The moon,
    The moon,
  They danced by the light of the moon.

Oscar Wilde

THE SELFISH GIANT

FROM

THE HAPPY PRINCE
AND OTHER STORIES

Illustrated by Greg Becker

Every afternoon, as they were coming from school, the children used to go and play in the Giant's garden.

It was a large lovely garden, with soft green grass. Here and there over the grass stood beautiful flowers like stars, and there were twelve peach-trees that in the spring-time broke out into delicate blossoms of pink and pearl, and in the autumn bore rich fruit. The birds sat on the trees and sang so sweetly that the children used to stop their games in order to listen to them. 'How happy we are here!' they cried to each other.

One day the Giant came back. He had been to visit his friend the Cornish ogre, and had stayed with him for seven years. After the seven years were over he had said all that he had to say, for his conversation was limited, and he determined to return to his own castle. When he arrived he saw the children playing in the garden.

'What are you doing here?' he cried in a very gruff voice, and the children ran away.

'My own garden is my own garden,' said the Giant; 'anyone can understand that, and I will allow nobody to play in it but myself.' So he built a high wall all round it, and put up a notice-board.

> TRESPASSERS
> WILL BE
> PROSECUTED

He was a very selfish Giant.

The poor children had now nowhere to play. They tried to play on the road, but the road was very dusty and full of hard stones, and they did not like it. They used to wander round the high walls when their lessons were over, and talk about the beautiful garden inside. 'How happy we were there!' they said to each other.

Then the Spring came, and all over the country there were little blossoms and little birds. Only in the garden of the Selfish Giant it was still winter. The birds did not care to sing in it as there were no children, and the trees forgot to blossom. Once a beautiful flower put its head out from the grass, but when it saw the notice-board it was so sorry for the children that it slipped back into the ground again, and went off to sleep. The only people who were pleased were the Snow and the Frost. 'Spring has forgotten this garden,' they cried, 'so we will live here all the year round.' The Snow covered up the grass with her great white cloak, and the Frost painted all the trees silver. Then they invited the North Wind to stay with them, and he came. He was wrapped in furs, and he roared all day about the garden, and blew the chimney pots down. 'This is a delightful spot,' he said, 'we must ask the Hail on a visit.' So the Hail came. Every day for three hours he rattled on the roof of the castle till he broke most of the slates, and then he ran round and round the garden as fast as he could go. He was dressed in grey, and his breath was like ice.

'I cannot understand why the Spring

is so late in coming,' said the Selfish Giant, as he sat at the window and looked out at his cold, white garden; 'I hope there will be a change in the weather.'

But the Spring never came, nor the Summer. The Autumn gave golden fruit to every garden, but to the Giant's garden she gave none. 'He is too selfish,' she said. So it was always winter there, and the North Wind and the Hail, and the Frost, and the Snow danced about through the trees.

One morning the Giant was lying awake in bed when he heard some lovely music. It sounded so sweet to his ears that he thought it must be the King's musicians passing by. It was really only a little linnet singing outside his window, but it was so long since he had heard a bird sing in his garden that it seemed to him to be the most beautiful music in the world. Then the Hail stopped dancing over his head, and the North Wind ceased roaring, and a delicious perfume came to him through the open casement. 'I believe the Spring has come at last,' said the Giant; and he jumped out of bed and looked out.

What did he see?

He saw a most wonderful sight. Through a little hole in the wall the children had crept in, and they were sitting in the branches of the trees. In every tree that he could see there was a little child. And the trees were so glad to have the children back again that they had covered themselves with blossoms, and were waving their arms gently above the children's heads. The birds were flying about and twittering with delight, and the flowers were looking up through the green grass and laughing. It was a lovely scene, only in one corner it was still winter. It was the farthest corner of the garden, and in it was standing a little boy. He was so small that he could not reach up to the branches of the tree, and he was wandering all round it, crying bitterly. The poor tree was still covered with frost and snow, and the North Wind was blowing and roaring above it. 'Climb up! little boy,' said the Tree, and it bent its branches down as low as it could but the boy was too tiny.

And the Giant's heart melted as he looked out. 'How selfish I have been!' he said: 'now I know why the Spring would not come here. I

will put that poor little boy on the top of the tree, and then I will knock down the wall, and my garden shall be the children's playground for ever and ever.' He was really very sorry for what he had done.

So he crept downstairs and opened the front door quite softly, and went out into the garden. But when the children saw him they were so frightened that they all ran away, and the garden became winter again. Only the little boy did not run for his eyes were so full of tears that he did not see the Giant coming. And the Giant stole up behind him and took him gently in his hand, and put him up into the tree. And the tree broke at once into blossom, and the birds came and sang on it, and the little boy stretched out his two arms and flung them round the Giant's neck, and kissed him. And the other children when they saw that the Giant was not wicked any longer, came running back, and with them came the Spring. 'It is your garden now, little children,' said the Giant, and he took a great axe and knocked down the wall. And when the people were going to market at twelve o'clock they found the Giant playing with the children in the most beautiful garden they had ever seen.

All day long they played, and in the evening they came to the Giant to bid him good-bye.

'But where is your little companion?' he said: 'the boy I put into the tree.' The Giant loved him the best because he had kissed him.

'We don't know,' answered the children: 'he has gone away.'

'You must tell him to be sure and come tomorrow,' said the Giant. But the children said that they did not know where he lived and had never seen him before; and the Giant felt very sad.

Every afternoon, when school was over, the children came and played with the Giant. But the little boy whom the Giant loved was never seen again. The Giant was very kind to all the children, yet he longed for his first little friend, and often spoke of him. 'How

I would like to see him!' he used to say.

Years went over, and the Giant grew very old and feeble. He could not play about any more, so he sat in a huge armchair, and watched the children at their games, and admired his garden. 'I have many beautiful flowers,' he said; 'but the children are the most beautiful flowers of all.'

One winter morning he looked out of his window as he was dressing. He did not hate the Winter now, for he knew that it was merely the Spring asleep, and that the flowers were resting.

Suddenly he rubbed his eyes in wonder and looked and looked. It certainly was a marvellous sight. In the farthest corner of the garden was a tree quite covered with lovely white blossoms. Its branches were golden, and silver fruit hung down from them, and underneath it stood the little boy he had loved.

Downstairs ran the Giant in great joy, and out into the garden. He hastened across the grass, and came near to the child. And when he came quite close his face grew red with anger, and he said, 'Who hath dared to wound thee?' For on the palms of the child's hands were the prints of two nails, and the prints of two nails were on the little feet.

'Who hath dared to wound thee?' cried the Giant, 'tell me, that I may take my big sword and slay him.'

'Nay,' answered the child: 'but these are the wounds of Love.'

'Who art thou?' said the Giant, and a strange awe fell on him, and he knelt before the little child.

And the child smiled on the Giant, and said to him, 'You let me play once in your garden, today you shall come with me to my garden, which is Paradise.'

And when the children ran in that afternoon, they found the Giant lying dead under the tree, all covered with white blossoms.

Alfred, Lord Tennyson

FROM

THE LADY OF SHALOTT

Illustrated by Alison Jay

On either side the river lie
Long fields of barley and of rye,
That clothe the wold and meet the sky;
And thro' the field the road runs by
   To many-tower'd Camelot;
And up and down the people go,
Gazing where the lilies blow
Round an island there below,
   The island of Shalott.

Willows whiten, aspens quiver,
Little breezes dusk and sliver
Thro' the wave that runs for ever
By the island in the river
   Flowing down to Camelot.
Four grey walls, and four grey towers,
Overlook a space of flowers,
And the silent isle embowers
   The Lady of Shalott.

By the margin, willow-veil'd,
Slide the heavy barges trail'd
By slow horses; and unhail'd
The shallop flitteth, silken-sail'd
   Skimming down to Camelot:
But who hath seen her wave her hand?
Or at the casement seen her stand?
Or is she known in all the land,
   The Lady of Shalott?

Only reapers, reaping early
In among the bearded barley,
Hear a song that echoes cheerly
From the river winding clearly,
   Down to tower'd Camelot:
And by the moon the reaper weary,
Piling sheaves in uplands airy,
Listening, whispers, ''Tis the fairy
   Lady of Shalott.'

Alfred, Lord Tennyson

THE CHARGE OF THE LIGHT BRIGADE

Illustrated by Gino D'Achille

I

Half a league, half a league,
 Half a league onward,
All in the valley of Death
 Rode the six hundred.
'Forward, the Light Brigade!
Charge for the guns!' he said;
Into the valley of Death
 Rode the six hundred.

II

'Forward, the Light Brigade!'
Was there a man dismay'd?
Not tho' the soldier knew
 Some one had blunder'd:
Their's not to make reply,
Their's not to reason why,
Their's but to do and die:
Into the valley of Death
 Rode the six hundred.

III

Cannon to right of them,
Cannon to left of them,
Cannon in front of them
  Volley'd and thunder'd;
Storm'd at with shot and shell,
Boldly they rode and well,
Into the jaws of Death,
Into the mouth of Hell
  Rode the six hundred.

IV

Flash'd all their sabres bare,
Flash'd as they turn'd in air,
Sabring the gunners there,
Charging an army, while
  All the world wonder'd:
Plunged in the battery-smoke
Right thro' the line they broke;
Cossack and Russian
Reel'd from the sabre-stroke
  Shatter'd and sunder'd.
Then they rode back, but not,
  Not the six hundred.

V

Cannon to right of them,
Cannon to left of them,
Cannon behind them
  Volley'd and thunder'd;
Storm'd at with shot and shell,
While horse and hero fell,
They that had fought so well
Came thro' the jaws of Death
Back from the mouth of Hell,
All that was left of them,
  Left of six hundred.

VI

When can their glory fade?
O the wild charge they made!
  All the world wonder'd.
Honour the charge they made!
Honour the Light Brigade,
  Noble six hundred!

Christina Rossetti

WHO HAS SEEN THE WIND?

Illustrated by Ruth Rivers

Who has seen the wind?
Neither I nor you:
But when the leaves hang trembling,
The wind is passing through.

Who has seen the wind?
Neither you nor I:
But when the trees bow down their heads,
The wind is passing by.

I give you the end of a golden string,
Only wind it into a ball,
It will lead you in at Heaven's gate
Built in Jerusalem's wall.

WILLIAM BLAKE

INDEX OF AUTHORS